Praise for the Author

"Alan Dean Foster is the modern-day Renaissance writer, as his abilities seem to have no genre boundaries."

—Bookbrowser for *The Mocking Program*

"One of the most consistently inventive and fertile writers of science-fiction and fantasy."

—The Times (London)

"Alan Dean Foster is a master of creating alien worlds for his protagonists to deal with."

—SFRevu for *Sagramanda*

"Foster's greatest strength remains his world building, easily creating evocative alien landscapes and populating them...."

—Booklist for *Strange Music*

"Amusing ... intriguing ... consistently entertaining."

—Locus for *Lost and Found*

"A winner for all ages."

           —*Publisher's Weekly* for *Lost and Found*

"Packed with action, intriguing human and alien characters, and a message of strength through diversity."

           —*Library Journal* for *Drowning World*

"Surefire entertainment … the author's mastery of his exotic setting cannot be denied."

           —*Publisher's Weekly* for *Drowning World*

"Inventive and packed with flavorsome incident."

           —*Kirkus Review* for *Carnivores of Light and Darkness*

THE FLAVORS OF OTHER WORLDS

THE FLAVORS OF OTHER WORLDS

13 Science Fiction Tales from a Master Storyteller

ALAN DEAN FOSTER

WFP
WordFire Press

Contents

Introduction

Alan Dean Foster
Prescott, Arizona
June, 2018

A few years ago, at the behest of some friends and relatives, I took a stab at starting an autobiography. It never got very far, mostly because I found it odd to be writing about myself. The proposed autobiography was called *Wanderings*.

Eventually it morphed to become *Predators I Have Known* (Open Road Media), a book about some of my travels. It was a good deal more fun to write about animal encounters than how a high school teacher named Solomon helped shape my future or how a water pistol my grandfather bought for me at age four suggested an eventual career choice.

All I ever wanted to do in life was travel. Restricted as I am to one small planet, I determined to see as much of it as possible. For this I largely blame Carl Barks and his creation Scrooge McDuck. When I was very young (three or four) my parents bought me subscriptions to about a dozen monthly comic books. There were no comic book stores, let alone comic conventions, and I was plainly far too young to be picking anything out of racks at newsstands (you can research these wonderful relics of ancient history, and you see them regularly in old movies). I learned to read via comic books.

Of which my favorite by far was Uncle Scrooge. Despite being old, having to use a cane, wear glasses, and having memory problems, Scrooge wandered the world in search of adventure (and profit). Even as a very young child I perceived via this comic character that anyone could see the world no matter their age. I determined that when I was old enough to do so, I would emulate Scrooge. I did not foresee that it would lead to a career as a writer, far less one focused on speculative fiction.

When I discovered science-fiction, through a couple of books my father kept, I was both enthralled (Asimov's collection *Nine Tomorrows*) and intimidated (Van Vogt's *World of Null-A*). I put SF aside for a while while I focused on academics and the classics, not returning to science-fiction until my senior year in high school. That was when I realized that via SF I could wander not only this one world but dozens, hundreds of others. I began to do so, starting with the classic Groff Conklin and Judith Merrell collections and moving on to individual novels. As a senior at UCLA I began to imagine new worlds of my own.

Now here I am today: still wandering, both on this world and in the hundreds of others in my mind, occasionally describing them for others to share. As much as I enjoy pointing out Bellini's last sculpture in Rome or a particularly interesting bug in Peru's Manu, I take pleasure in detailing a planet-wide rainforest in *Midworld* or one based on slime in the forthcoming *Secretions*. It all harkens back to Barks and Scrooge.

On the first page of Barks' Scrooge adventure *The Mines of King Solomon*, a frantic Scrooge is preparing for his annual tour of his international properties. While dictating instructions to his army of subordinates, he recites a litany of utterly fascinating place names that Barks doubtless drew from his file of old National Geographic magazines. My favorite was Famagusta, which for years I thought surely must be an invented name for a made-up place. When I discovered that it was a real location, I determined one day to go there.

Famagusta is an old city on Cyprus. There aren't a lot of tourists, it's a fun place to wander around, and there are a couple of little cafes and one decent souvenir shop. My thanks to Barks and Scrooge for the heads-up.

I hope you get to Famagusta some day. In the interim, here are some more wanderings, to places and times and worlds that I've enjoyed making up for myself, and am pleased to share.

1

Unvasion

Guns and bombs, or spears and arrows, or rocks and clubs: all variations on the same theme, and all of them outdated. Why, historically, has one country, or tribe, or fiefdom sought to overthrow another? To control its population and its resources, of course. But if you embark on a Thirty Year's War, or a Hundred Year's War, or a World War, one side not only ends up destroying the opposing population and resources it desires to control but also inevitably impoverishing itself.

It's just not a very cost-effective way to conquer.

Yet nation-states are still stuck in the same mindset. Destroy, overpower, obliterate. Everyone has seen one of a thousand variations on the cartoon of a single surviving soldier standing alone amidst total destruction and crying out, "I won!" Won what? Scorched earth?

Some aspects of society are finally growing more sophisticated where such enterprises are concerned. That doesn't mean that some newcomers might not have more experience in such matters and be better at it.

Aliens, for example. With better credit scores.

IT ALL BEGAN when the L'treth indicated their desire to acquire a McDonald's franchise.

Yes.

As an experienced executive assistant and qualified paralegal, Karen possessed an exhaustive assortment of expressions, but the one she flashed Noble when she entered his office was new to him. "I thought I'd come and tell you in person, Derrick. I *wanted* to come and tell you in person." Her gaze flicked ever so briefly backward, in the direction of the outer office. "There are two aliens waiting to see you. They're causing something of a stir."

Noble had been a lawyer far too long to let anything, anything at all, unsettle him. Especially so early in the morning. "Do tell. Well, I guess you'd better send them in before the stir becomes a ruckus." He glanced at a desk calendar and exhaled slowly. "I'm free 'til eleven. Hold the Harrington department store group half an hour if you have to."

"Yes, sir."

She disappeared momentarily. In her wake there eventually appeared a pair of L'treth. They studied the office with interest and, Noble chose to believe, approval. "Won't you come in—gentlemen," he added after a moment's indecision. The L'treth were hard to sex. "Please, take a seat."

The aliens were short, squat, horizontal of eye, and broad of nose and mouth. Frog-like, according to the popular media, but not intimidatingly so. Any superficial batrachian resemblance ended there. Their shimmering, silvery skin was smooth to the point of looking polished, their attire colorful and varied according to individual taste, and they were reassuringly bipedal. The fold of delicate, fluted flesh that crossed their otherwise bald heads weaved slowly back and forth like kelp off the California coast. The single hearing organ was no less offensive to the general aesthetic than were humankind's dual, projecting, wrinkled ears. Only their limbs smacked of the truly exotic: a pair of supple three-foot long pseudopods that terminated in flexible, black-rimmed suckers. As the L'treth sat down they rested these, not on their hind limbs, but by draping them back over their shoulders and crossing them behind their short necks. Not only was this posture intriguing, to a human it was also demonstrably non-threatening: the equivalent of putting one's hands behind one's back.

"I am J'mard," the slightly larger alien began, without further delay. The L'treth were known to have a horror of wasting time. "We understand that you are given to taking atypical assignments, Mr. Noble." J'mard's English was flawless. In consequence of their wondrous talent for aural mimicry, not to mention flexible larynxes, the L'treth easily mastered whatever Earthly language they chose to study. Conversely, a human could speak L'treth, but it required a good deal of effort. Even then, the experts had trouble with pronunciation and grammar.

"I like a challenge," Noble admitted readily. "I've been a lawyer for a long time, and I'm easily bored."

"I am N'delk," declared the other. Reaching into a pouch made of some sumptuous metallic material slung at his short waist, he handed his host a thumbnail-sized cube. "Please to insert this into your computer. I assure you, it will do it no harm, nor will it plant anything intrusive. We do not injure those whose advice we seek."

Noble hesitated only briefly before popping the cube into the less essential of the two machines on his desk. Something loaded instantly, and he was rewarded with a spray of diagrams and figures. Captions were rendered both in English and in the complex L'treth script. Noble recognized surveyor plats almost as soon as he did the familiar yellow arch.

"This shows a plot of land at the junction of Interstate 17 and New River Road in the central part of the American state of Arizona," J'mard explained. "We think it would be an excellent location for a McDonald's."

N'delk's hearing organ fluttered. "Humans would flock to it. We calculate that it would return an admirable profit."

Noble studied the monitor for a while, then nodded. "I agree. Not really my specialty, but to my casual eyes it looks like a good site." Turning away from the monitor, he met large, limpid gray eyes. "The first question that occurs to me is; what do the L'treth need with monetary profit? Or for that matter, Earthly currency of any kind?"

J'mard replied. "Since the time of First Contact, which was not so very long ago, many of us visiting your world have expressed a desire to work with your kind in the evolution of ventures of mutual interest. Your world has much to offer the L'treth, in the form of opportunities for mutual manufacturing, tourism, the acquisition of your wonderful handicrafts, and so on. In order to do this, those of us who are interested require access to quantities of the local medium of exchange.

"The best way for us to obtain such currency is to participate in your dominant free-enterprise form of commerce. This means entering into and participating in the local business community. Making investments. Dumping valued items easily obtainable elsewhere, such as gold or hard, clear carbon, would only weaken your economic system. Not only do we have no desire to do this, but it would be counter to what we seek to achieve. We hope to work within the framework of your existing economic system without causing it any harm."

"Very thoughtful of you," Noble admitted. "I can, of course, represent you in negotiations for the land, and for the acquisition of the franchise. Where will you get the currency to pay for them?"

Opening his own pouch, N'delk brought forth a sucker full of small metal needles. They glittered and danced in the light of Derrick Noble's office. "We can offer access to certain technologies that your scientists and researchers are tracking, but have not yet perfected. Inserting one of these into a human body will kill any runaway cell development that is present. To prevent the development of dangerous economic jealousies, we intend to make this simultaneously available to more than a single company."

Noble stared at the innocuous little needles that had suddenly assumed an importance all out of proportion to their appearance or size. "In other words, they are a cure for cancer."

"Generally. They are not omnipotent." N'delk was nothing if not earnest. "Do they constitute a suitable initial offering, or should we retire and attempt to bring forth an alternative?"

Noble's brows were as gray as the eyes of the L'treth. They arched as he focused on the needles. "No, I don't think that will be necessary. You will be amply compensated by several companies in return for the rights to exploit the properties of these ... devices. So much so that I can't help but wonder why you need a McDonald's franchise."

The aliens exchanged a glance and a murmur before N'delk replied. "As we have told you, we wish to participate in your commerce. Imposing from above is not participation." He held out the needles. "There is a limit to how much technology we can offer that your kind would find useful."

Among other skills he had acquired in thirty years of practicing law, Noble had learned how to make rapid decisions. Rising, he extended a hand. "Mr. J'mard, Mr. N'delk, I am delighted to inform you that you are now represented, at least in the state of Arizona in the country of the United States of America, by accredited legal counsel."

THE L'TRETH WERE RIGHT. With its carefully chosen location, their new McDonald's prospered. The parent corporation was equally pleased, as any company is when someone franchising its product expands its customer base. They were so pleased that when another pair of L'treth, desiring to emulate the local success of their pioneering brethren, applied for a franchise in North Carolina, it was immediately granted. Since franchise territories did not overlap, their human counterparts had no objection to the aliens' success. After all, general sales contributed to the overall earnings of the national company, whose success in turn benefited all franchisees.

The L'treth were model operators, their restaurants clean and well-run. They were particularly appreciated by their teenage part-time help, who when back in school could boast of working for aliens off-hours or over the summer—even though the L'treth relied on their human managers and were rarely seen on site. The consequences, of course, were inevitable and easily foreseen. It was only a matter of time before a consortium of ten L'treth applied for several Burger King franchises in the Northeast.

The fad, if that was what it could be called, spread rapidly. Within a year, L'treth could be found owning and operating fast food restaurants, commercial websites, flower shops (they were especially fond of flowers, it developed), shoe stores, candy outlets, dry cleaners, car washes, and all manner of businesses not only in the US, but throughout the world. Naturally, the French held out longest against this new kind of foreign ownership, but when the L'treth began operating within the borders of the EEC, there was nothing the French could legally do to keep them out.

What was the point, anyway? The aliens brought with them injections of fresh capital, created new jobs, and were model operators who invariably (but not always) deferred to the recommendations of their human managers. L'treth-owned businesses contributed to regional charities, sponsored youth football teams, and were assiduous boosters of local chambers-of-commerce. True, they looked funny, but so did those guys from Kalamazoo who operated the biggest chain of auto-parts stores in the eastern US. Really, people were fond of saying, what was the difference between off-shore ownership based in Budapest and off-world ownership based on L'treth?

That's why the bombing caught everyone by surprise.

It happened in Sydney, of all places. Hardly the city one would pick as a hotbed of economic terrorism. The target was one of a chain of L'treth-owned pharmacies. The bombers called in the details of their plan to a local radio station, in order to give customers and staff of the intended target plenty of time to get out. The warning ended with a clarion cry: "People of Earth—Rise Up Against Your Alien Masters!"

It had a nice, defiant ring to it, but to most people it smacked of anarchy and idiocy. The L'treth were masters of nothing. If anything, they had gone out of their way to be good corporate citizens, in many instances far better than the humans whose financial participation they had supplanted. They had proven on numerous occasions that they could not be bribed, and they were exemplary custodians of the environment.

So what if the L'treth owned a majority share of Gazprom, or Apple, or Shell? Who cared if they made money off Hyundai or BHP? Their profits were inevitably reinvested, to the benefit of the companies they controlled and the employees who worked for them. They were working entirely within the local economic system, without harming it in any way.

Those who complained about nebulous, indefinable "alien influences" were demoted. The L'treth did not even have to fire anyone. Employees who grew too noisy found themselves transferred to remote locations. A few, defiant to the end, quit and moved to the deep woods. Their fellow humans thought them eccentric and harmless, as they always had those of iconoclastic bent.

The L'treth bought car manufacturers and food processors, information distributors and entertainment enterprises. Every purchase was scrupulously studied for antitrust violations, or for violations of local ordinances in whatever country the transaction was taking place. Where competition continued to exist, no one could find grounds for complaint. In point of fact, the L'treth encouraged competition: it was good for business.

Twenty years later, Noble was honored by a surprise visit from J'mard. Through dint of hard work and clever investment, the alien was now the local equivalent of a minor billionaire. Noble welcomed him readily—his association with the L'treth had seen him included very early on in the chain of spiraling profitability.

"What can I do for you, my friend?"

"Nothing, Derrick." J'mard chose one of the new chairs, plush and expensive, and struggled to raise his closer-to-the-ground-than-human backside up onto it. "I just thought to pay you a friendly visit."

"You're always welcome in my office or my home. You know that." The lawyer proffered an open box of fine Cuban cigars. J'mard took one, neatly bit off the end, chewed, swallowed, and took another bite, content.

Noble closed the box and set it back on his desk. His walking cane rested on the other side, but he disdained it. He was feeling good this morning. "Can I help you make an acquisition, J'mard? Anything new on the agenda?" Not that he needed the money, not anymore. At his age, it was the challenge inherent in the work that continued to excite Noble.

The alien munched daintily on the fragrant, finely rolled tobacco and gestured with one sucker-tipped limb. "I wish you could, Derrick, but there doesn't seem to be much left to buy."

The lawyer chuckled. "You don't own everything, you know. You've done well, but you don't control everything."

"Enough. The rest will fall into place more slowly, but fall it will."

Noble blinked. "I'm not sure I follow you, J'mard."

"Why, the rest of the invasion, of course. You inevitably reach a point where things slow down, but they still proceed. They are proceeding nicely. Well ahead of schedule, really." He ventured the broad L'treth equivalent of a smile. For some reason, today Noble did not find it engaging.

"What invasion?" The elderly lawyer frowned. "You're not referring to that hostile takeover of United Biscuits your British subsidiary attempted last month, are you?"

J'mard's expression rippled. Much like humans, the L'treth possessed an elaborate language of facial expressions. "The subjugation of your world, of course. It is a scenario we have repeated, with consistent success, on a number of worlds. It is always the easiest way to go about it. What is the point of blowing up cities and annihilating populations? What is to be gained, when the radioactive dust has settled?" He bit off another piece of cigar. "Highly counterproductive."

"You don't control anything but companies," Noble pointed out, feeling suddenly uneasy. "Anytime humans wanted, they could rise up and kick you out. I don't mean to be brusque with an old friend, but that's the truth."

The hearing organ fluttered like a tangoing jellyfish. "I'm glad you think of me as a friend. I think of you that way too, Derrick. No one will rise up who has a good job and is afraid of losing it. What is the difference in who one works for, be it L'treth or human? A boss is a boss. And we are good bosses. Everyone prospers under us. We simply like to be in control."

"But you're not," Noble protested. This was not the discussion he'd anticipated having when J'mard's arrival had been announced. He had thought they would talk about golf.

J'mard admired the marvelous view beyond the office windows. "Do you know how much money we gave to the Republican Party last year? Both to the party, and to individuals running for office? To the Democrats? To the New Tsarists in Russia and the Liberals in Britain? To the resurrected Falun Gong in China? It is standard procedure among human businesses, of course, to contribute to a great many causes, social as well as political. We control what we need to control, and that control is getting stronger every day. There is no shame in it, and no harm. Humans do not care who runs their governments and businesses, so long as they are well run. And as you know, the L'treth are very efficient."

"You could be exposed any day." Noble wondered why he was arguing. It was the lawyer in him, he decided. The old debater. "Anyone with determination and knowledge could expose you. *I* could expose you."

"Could you, Derrick? You know that we own fifty-five percent of the company that operates this law firm."

His jaw dropped. "No. No, I didn't know that."

"Shadow corporation operating from the Caymans," the alien explained blithely. "Please, old friend, do not look so alarmed. We have no intention of firing you. Besides, we own large stakes in many newspaper and magazine and television and internet groups. You would find it a hard time getting your message out. If you succeeded, our media people would act to quickly marginalize it."

"People would respond. Enough would see through the obfuscation, and understand, and rise up. Humans are devoted to their independence."

J'mard made a sound indicative of quiet disagreement. "Humans love their jobs, and their vacation time, and their professional sports, and their television and films and tabloid newspapers. When they have these, independence is reduced to a philosophical abstract that holds little meaning for the human on the street." He fought to edge himself further back into the chair. "We really must play some golf again. A fascinating game, though because of our short stature we are somewhat at a disadvantage compared to you, its inventors." Pseudopods waved. "But we are excellent putters, are we not?" Giving up on the chair, he slid back to the floor. Noble could do nothing but stare at him.

"Bombs and death-rays—who needs them? Come with me to Florida this weekend, Derrick. N'delk will be there, and we can play through the new Woods-designed course at Sarasota. You'll like it. It's owned by the Malaysian branch of one of our newest companies." Having mastered, like so many other aspects of human society, the culture of the handshake, he extended a forelimb at the end of which there was no hand.

Not really knowing what else to do, not really seeing an alternative, Noble took it. "I don't care what you say or how you attempt to rationalize it, it all comes down to semantics. No matter what you do, no matter what you try, you'll never conquer us."

"Conquer you?" The squat, stocky alien looked up at him out of soft gray eyes. "Why should we want to try and conquer you? Humans are tough, skilled, highly adaptable fighters. We recognized that right away. In a fight, you would be hard to defeat. Even with the kind of advanced technology we have shared with you, a war would be difficult to win." Had J'mard possessed eyelids, Noble was certain he would have winked.

"Besides, why would we want to damage that which we already own?"

2

The Man Who Knew Too Much

*R*ay Bradbury, *author of* Fahrenheit 451, *among other wonderful books, once said that the library was his church. Nowadays we have many more ways to worship. eBooks and browsing the internet have changed the way we absorb knowledge.*

For many people it wouldn't matter if all that went away. Most folk are happy to be told what to do and how to do it, and are satisfied with a regular paycheck (see: "Unvasion"). But for the rest of us, it's not sufficient just to know the minimum necessary. We want to know more. We need to know more, even if that particular knowing has no immediate or even potential usefulness. We crave strings of words that when taken as a whole provide us with information, enlightenment, entertainment.

Why, you're subject to that affliction right now....

"PSSST ... wanna buy some real *hard* stuff?"

Charlie Fellows paused. It was late, he was on his way home, and the alcove the voice emerged from was very dark. Still, he hesitated. Buying stuff on the street was always chancy. You didn't know if what you were getting was pure and undiluted or just a cheap knock-off from Taipei or Shanghai. The latter might consist of nothing more than a couple of cursory introductions and a table of contents followed by hours of listings scanned from the local telephone books.

Night damp wafting in off the Pacific teased his lips with a chill burning. He clutched the collar of his coat tighter around his neck. It was cold. The familiar throbbing had already started at the back of his head, demanding attention. Demanding to be fed. A quick glance to left and then right revealed that the narrow side street off University was deserted. Not surprising, at this hour. He licked slightly chapped lips and gave in. Telling himself he could resist the urge never worked.

"What—what've you got?"

A thin crescent of Cheshire Cat ivory, the ghost of a grin, appeared in the darkness. Nimble fingers brought forth and manipulated a flat, rectangular, maroon-tinged plastic container that resembled a woman's oversized compact. A single internal LEP illuminated half a dozen rows of neatly aligned chipets. Each was no bigger than his little fingernail. Charlie eyed them hungrily.

"What did I tell you? All uncontaminated, newly pressed, and unabridged. Straight from the relevant authorized sources."

Charlie's eyes widened slightly as he leaned forward to inspect the glistening array. They glittered like miniature Christmas ornaments. He could not conceal his eagerness. "Looks good. Clean. Where'd you get 'em?"

It was the wrong thing to say, and he knew it as soon as he said it. The case snapped shut with a soft airtight *pop*. "Sorry, man, I guess I had you scoped wrong. You take care now, and …"

Charlie put out an anxious hand to forestall the younger man's departure. "No, wait—I'm sorry. That was a dumb thing to say."

"Yeah, it was." One hand on the alcove's dark door, the sallow-faced pusher paused.

"It just slipped out." Desperately, Charlie mustered his most ingratiating smile. "Let me—can I see the stuff again?"

Still hugging the shadows, the pusher performed his own swift street survey. A quick flick of one fingertip and the case reopened. "What's your pleasure, citizen? What fires your interest?" Despite the tension inherent in the moment, his words floated on an undertone of mild amusement.

Charlie's response didn't disappoint. "Everything."

Nodding, the pusher's finger traced the air over the shimmering chipets, as if by so doing he could command them to rise from their holding sockets and perform a teasing little dance in midair. He was deliberately making Charlie wait, enjoying the other man's impatience. "Well now, I got here some natural science, some high-energy physics, a little general geology—but I prefer to specialize, you know? Mostly soft stuff tonight: American Lit, some archetypical anthropological Australian dreamtime studies, collections of arcane Melanesian oral traditions. Also a couple odds and ends." His hovering finger drifted over one corner of the case. "Maintenance manuals for Harley-Davidson models 1945-2005, the Complete Julia Childs' French Chef, Frescoes of the Northern Italian Renaissance." His knowing gaze bored into Charlie. "That last one's discontinued."

Charlie nodded eagerly, unable to take his eyes off the magical, gleaming little squares. No gem dealer in a back-alley Jaipur bazaar ever gazed with greater avarice upon an open handkerchief laden with jewels. "You said American Lit. You got Twain, Melville, Hawthorne?"

"Irving, Ferber, Poe—all the biggies. They're all here." Withdrawing specialized non-ferrous tweezers from a shirt pocket, he delicately plucked one chip from among the dozens and held it out toward his potential customer. "Have a look. First-class manufacture. Exactly what an authorized prof would use for broadcast."

Extracting the folding loupe he carried in one pocket, Charlie examined the chipet as best he could in the dim light. The miniscule factory identification markings looked genuine, but could he trust the provenance? His head throbbed. He'd been paid two days ago. He decided to take a chance.

Commerce concluded, the pusher vanished into the night. Charlie made no effort to see which way he went. Already, the freshly minted chipet was burning a hole in his pocket. Fired with expectation, he brushed past a few startled pedestrians on his way home, hardly seeing them. Had they taken the time to study his face, they might have recognized the eager, focused stare of an addict.

Once inside his apartment, the door safely bolted against the outside world, he changed into the terrycloth bathrobe rendered smooth by endless washings, made coffee, and readied himself. Out from its hidden compartment in the wall behind the Vienna Kunstmuseum poster came the eSnood. Working carefully, sensuously, he eased the lightweight plastic helmet with its embedded network of wires and transducers over his head, meticulously fine-tuning the fit. Worn too loose and he might miss whole short stories. Fastened too tight and it would squeeze his ears.

Though the illegal chipet was immediately accepted by the receptacle in the handset controller, he didn't relax until the familiar warmth began to steal over his thoughts. The pounding at the back of his head eased. The pusher had been as good as his word, as good as Charlie's money. This was the real thing. Snugging down into the crushed depths of the easy chair, sipping coffee by rote, Charlie lapsed easily and effortlessly into the contented semi-coma of someone soaking up hundreds of mental units via direct induction.

He didn't quit, he couldn't quit, until four in the morning, by which time he had absorbed the complete works of every great and numerous minor American fiction writer of the 18th and 19th centuries. Sated, exhausted, he wrestled his head out of the eSnood, staggered to the bedroom, and slept right through until suppertime. It cost him a day at work, but he didn't care. When queried by his superior, he would claim that illness had laid him low—which was not entirely untrue. It had been a near-perfect assimilation, smooth and virtually painless except for a persistent cramping in his right thigh. He felt the usual exhilaration, the classic thrill, the unmatchable mental high. Of becoming smarter, more erudite.

He had Gained Knowledge.

At work the following day his boss bawled him out good. Illness or no illness, he was told, he should have called in so his division could at least have brought in a temp for the day. Adrift in remembrances of works as diverse yet enthralling as *A Voyage to the South Seas*, *The Headless Horseman*, *Omoo*, and much, much more, Charlie didn't care. He took note of the stern tongue-lashing with half a mind. The remainder was still luxuriating in the memory of the effortless absorption of knowledge. The glow lasted all week.

By Saturday he needed another hit, and went looking for the pusher.

The chipets that university professors used to distribute material to their students contained enormous quantities of information that were supposed to be doled out gradually, by experts and specialists, in measured doses of information, properly footnoted and annotated. Their contents were not intended even for experienced instructors to absorb all at once. There was real danger involved in doing so; the threat of overloading the cerebral cortex, of swamping the brain's ability to process raw data.

But because it shouldn't be done, didn't mean it couldn't be.

Soft-spoken and polite, well-educated, a reliable toiler in Menlo Park's silicon alleys, Charlie Fellows was a knowledge addict. Ever since he had been exposed to the eSnood at a college party and the chipets it broadcast, the non-working portion of his adult life had been given over to learning, finding out, spending time in the acquisition of lore. When the ability to do so only slightly less than instantly, to suck up whole reams of learning overnight, had become scientifically possible if physically dangerous and culturally frowned upon, a small but thriving subculture had sprung up in its wake. Charlie had become an active member of that subculture very early on. It was an obsession he had in common with his closest friends, with Cheryl Chakula and Wayne Moorhead and C.K. Wang and Winona Gibson. Some of them he saw regularly at work, others he knew socially.

Like all of them, he was a knowledge junkie.

If the acquisition of erudition was your be all and end all, if it was your grail, your heart's desire, then no faster way had ever been devised to achieve it than through the use of the eSnood and the chipets that fueled it. Like information acquired by reading or viewing, once stored in the mind, data derived via inducted chipets stayed put. Charlie's brain was stuffed, swollen, crammed full of wondrous esoterica gleaned from night after night of reposing in his favorite chair while the eSnood pumped fact after fact through the neurons hiding under his hair. He knew more about salt water aquarium maintenance than any pet store manager. His ability to delineate the formulae for common sugars and proteins was the equal of innumerable highly-paid chemists on the payroll of Betty Crocker and Duncan Hines. He could recite quatrains whole and entire from medieval French poetry and discourse learnedly on the mechanics of moon rockets as well as bicycles. Only two dilemmas marred his artificially acquired scholarly bliss.

It wasn't enough. Ever.

And when he wasn't learning, his head began to hurt.

It was not as if no warnings existed. Every chipet manufactured for industrial or university use carried imprinted upon it in microscopic font the standard caveat: "The Surgeon General has warned that the assimilation of too much knowledge too rapidly can be hazardous to your health." At least once a week one of the major newscasts carried the story of some poor soul dead of an overdose on Proust or Hawking, African agricultural statistics or an attempt to digest the entire *Mahabharata* in one evening's sitting. What was news to the uncurious was not news to Charlie. He knew the risks from personal experience.

Just last year, his friend and company co-worker Dexter Ashburn had o.d'ed right on his florid and floral living room couch halfway through Manley's *Guide to the Echinoderms of the Western Pacific*. Sheree LeMars was still in rehab, recovering from an ill-conceived attempt to mainline *The Complete Fashions of the English Court: 1600-2000*. And then there was the sad, bad case of little Chesley Waycross. He was still recovering from the beating he'd received from a disgruntled customer. Ches' had tried to trade straight up for a copy of *Barrington's Ornithology of Brazil and Venezuela* with an unperused bootleg of *The Complete Litera-ture of 16th century Tibet*. Unfortunately, the chipet Chesley had offered in exchange had been bogus: there was no literature in 16th century Tibet. His enraged client had netted nothing but a standard pornset compilation; common, cheap, and useless. He'd taken out his anger and frustration on the unknowing Waycross.

One had to tread carefully on the street of knowledge.

Why not stop? he had once been challenged by an ex-girlfriend. Stop learning, he had replied? One might as well stop breathing. Hadn't Erasmus (whose complete writings Charlie had inhaled one night on a beautiful day in May) said that "To stop learning is to start to die"? Sure it was so, she had agreed, but with the eSnood and a tsunami of chipets, wasn't the reverse true?

Charlie didn't care. He only knew that from the time he had been old enough to read, the pursuit of knowledge had been the principal driving force in his life. If only we lived for thousand years or so there might be no need to try and cram so much information into so little time, he knew. But humans did not live for a thousand years. If you wanted to learn a little bit, a minimally respectable amount, really learn, then direct induction was the only way.

Ignorance could not be borne. It was unthinkable. Like his friends and fellow addicts, it wasn't simply that Charlie *wanted* to know. He *had* to know. *Needed* to know. Needed knowledge as urgently as he needed food, or water, or air. Otherwise, what was the meaning of life? Gobbling hamburgers and watching football? Mindless reproduction and the acquisition of false wealth? Far better to grasp the intricacies of diatom skeletons, the taxonomy of Southeast Asian flowers, the workings of the Aurora or the mysteries of zydeco music. So what if it killed you, eventually, by overloading your cranial capacity?

At least you would die knowing *something*.

They caught up with him eventually. If he'd moved away, he very likely would have escaped arrest, trial, incarceration, and imprisonment. But he loved where he lived, he liked his job, and besides, the best stuff was always to be found in the vicinity of major universities. Stanford was no exception. Given the scope of his personal chipet inventory and the extent of his addiction, the judge threw the book at him. This was not necessary, since he had long since inducted the complete civil code of the State of California. It did not help his defense, however.

He was sent to the *Northern California Center for the Treatment of the Data Addicted*, in Monterey. There, when he wasn't in lockdown and forced to watch endless hours of mind-purifying daytime television, he wandered the halls in the company of fellow compulsives: lapsed physicists from the heavily addicted part of Pasadena that bordered Cal-Tech, dour-faced recreational users caught hiding out with volumes of Balzac and African healer texts up in Humboldt County, softly mumbling immigrant programmers from Uttar Pradesh and Canton and Singapore. Shared verbalized snatches of Rabelais and Einstein and Cosell filled the hallways, repeated by the desperate inmates as self-sustaining mantras, but it wasn't enough, not near enough, to satisfy the information-starved like himself.

It was almost as tough as being forced to go cold turkey. In addition to television, the presence of daily newspapers, weekly magazines, and internet access provided the merest dribble of data, the feeblest kind of mental methadone. To someone used to ingesting the complete works of Shakespeare or *Mammals of Eastern Russia* or *Statistical Digest of Nebraska* in a few hours, it was the cerebral equivalent of providing nothing to drink for months on end but distilled water to a community comprised of seventy-year old Scotsmen.

Charlie pleaded. He wept, he raged, he implored. It was no use. Newspapers, magazines, tv, internet was all that was supplied. Information presented in the traditional manner: to the brain via the eyes, slowly, oh so slowly.

He got better. Withdrawal was painful, but he got better. Gradually he re-learned how to read a magazine: how to skip the advertisements, block out the irrelevant, and concentrate on the articles only. How to handle a newspaper again without avidly devouring the obituaries or the columns of sports statistics or the innumerable but still educational want ads. How to watch and enjoy television without— well, without doing much of anything. Slowly, he could feel his brain softening to something like tapioca pudding normal. The process of rehabilitation was made easier because during it all he retained everything he had absorbed through the use of his now confiscated eSnood and precious, priceless, irreplaceable chipets. He did not lose information already acquired; at least, no more than was typical. In data rehab, some leakage was inevitable.

When they felt he was sufficiently cured, they returned him to society. He was welcomed back at his job, for despite his boss's occasional outbursts, Charlie was regarded as a fine, competent worker who excelled at his craft and would willingly work long hours. Besides, by now everyone knew that he had been sick. He went about his daily activities with a new serenity, the result of the best treatment the State could provide. He went about them for weeks, and then for months, without a relapse. Went about them until he was sure he was no longer being monitored by the local police data division of Narcotics.

Only then did he once more begin to venture out to his old, familiar haunts in response to the lure of pure, undiluted, concentrated knowledge. His first buy since getting out of rehab was a wondrous compilation of the lives of the Mughals, translated from the original Sanskrit. Nestling back in his chair, the newly purchased, battered, but still serviceable second-hand eSnood resting awkwardly but satisfactorily on his head, he let himself lapse all over again into the sumptuous, sensuous sensation of effortlessly absorbing erudition. Of learning far faster than he ever could by the ancient eyescan method called reading. Of becoming more knowing. It might kill him, but he didn't care. We all die eventually anyway. Only, some of us die knowing more than others.

In a way, he felt badly for the authorities. All the courses of treatment they had devised, all the expensive programs and curriculum that had been developed with an eye toward curing the afflicted, couldn't really treat the root causes of the problem. Once one has become truly, madly, deeply addicted to the acquisition of knowledge, nothing else really satisfies. It was like any true craving: the more you have, the more you want. For the first time, where knowledge was concerned, the eSnood made it possible to completely indulge that compulsion.

It was mid-morning when old Aurangzeb, the last of the Mughals, finally passed into history and into the repository of Charlie Fellows' memory. With a languid sigh of complete satisfaction that bordered on the prurient, Charlie blinked and tenderly removed the plasticized network of induction contacts from his head. A glance at the clock showed that he had missed another day of work. He didn't care. He now knew all about Akbar and Shah Jahan and their most interesting ilk, and felt much the better for it. The more *knowledgeable*. The pounding at the back of his head was no worse than tolerable. He felt fine. Infused. Educated. There was only one problem. As always. As there ever would be.

He was still thirsty.

3

Perception

---

*Y*ou can't hurry love, no you'll just have to wait...." So sang the Supremes.

As humans we have been able to quantify a good many things. Love is not one of them. It remains as mysterious and fascinating as it ever was, likely since before the dawn of civilization.

Unfailingly, we all remember our first love. The tingle of attraction, the over-whelming desire to join with another, the temptations inherent in giving oneself wholly to another person. We also equally remember the first time we were in love and were rejected. The hurt, the pain, the feelings of worthlessness.

But in the latter instance, what does the rejector feel? Regret? Apology? Sympathy? Anything at all? In the coldness of adolescence, often nothing.

It is left to the rejected to feel.

(Note: "Perception" appears here in its original form for the first time.)

STEFAN DIDN'T WANT the assignment to Irelis. He didn't want to work at the Outpost. He'd seen pictures of Irelis, and the Outpost, and the natives, and found all of them unpleasant in equal measure. But advancing up the company ladder meant climbing the rungs in order. Maybe skipping one now and then, if you were fortunate. For a young apprentice such as himself, Irelis was a rung that couldn't be skipped.

So it was that he found himself installed at the Outpost, a self-contained subdivision of the larger Irelis station set in the middle of a swamp. It could as easily have been anywhere on Irelis except at the poles. Swamp or savanna, take your choice: they were what covered nearly all of Irelis except for the murky, algae-coated oceans. Of the two, the savannas offered the more pleasant prospect, with drier, cooler, weather. Unfortunately, humans weren't the only ones who preferred the plains to the swamps. So did the several dozen species of ferocious biting arthropods that sucked body fluids without discriminating between planets of origin.

The Allawout got around the swamps on primitive flat rafts fashioned from fiberthrush and covango saplings fastened together with strong, red looporio vine. Ages ago, some Allawout Einstein had figured out that if you built the rafts with points at both ends, not only would they go faster through the tepid, turgid water, but you wouldn't have to turn them around to reverse direction. That discovery represented the height of Allawout nautical technology. The idea of a sail was beyond them. Ignoring directives that forbade supplying indigenous aliens with advanced knowledge, visiting humans who observed the locals struggling with poles and paddles had taken pity on them and introduced the concept of the rudder, an innovation that the natives readily adopted and for which they were inordinately grateful.

To the Outpost they brought the pleasures and treasures of the Irelis hinterlands; unique organic gem material, seeds from which exotic spices were extracted, sustainable animal products, barks and resins and flowers from which were derived uniquely unsynthesizable pharmaceuticals, and their own fashionable primitive handicrafts. Widely scattered and hard to find, located in disagreeable, dangerous country, these diverse products of Irelis found their way into the insatiable current of interstellar trade through the good offices of the dirt (literally) poor natives. Everyone benefited, and the government was happy.

Stefan was not happy. He did not quite hate Irelis, but he disliked the place intensely. For someone his age, there was nothing in the way of entertainment. Worst of all was having to work with the locals. None of the Allawout stood taller than a meter in height—if you could call it standing. In the absence of anything resembling legs or feet, it was hard to tell. They sort of slimed their way along, their listless pace in perfect harmony with their sluggish metabolisms. A quartet of narrow but strong tentacles protruded from their cephalopodian upper bodies. These were covered in a fine, hairless, slick skin not unlike that of a frog or salamander. From the center of the upper bulge that was not quite a proper head, two large round eyes marked by crescent-shaped pupils took in the swamp that was their whole wide world. They had no external ears, no fur or horns, and wore no clothing. Not that there was much to cover. When they burbled at one another in their crude, vowel-rich language, bubbles frothed at the corners of their lipless mouths. They had no proper teeth and subsisted on a wide variety of soft plant life, supplementing this with the occasional fresh-water mollusk that did not require over-much chewing. Soon after arriving, Stefan had the opportunity to observe them eating. It was not a pretty sight.

It did not take him long to learn from his three co-workers that the Allawout were as oblivious to human sarcasm as they were too much of the world around them. Making fun of the slow-moving, slow-thinking natives was one of the few spontaneous diversions available to the Outpost's inhabitants. Except when a supervisor came visiting, it was a sport they indulged in shamelessly, taking care to do so only out of range of the station's largely humorless scientific compliment. By the time Stefan's tour of duty was half over, his own personal file of Allawout jokes had grown as fat as one of the natives.

Not that they were inherently unlikable, he mused as he lazed his way through his daily turn at the trading counter. On his right was a projector that could, magically as far as the Allawout were concerned, generate a three-dimensional, rotatable image of anything in the Outpost's warehouse. Those visiting natives who made endless demands of the device simply for its entertainment value soon found themselves cut out of the trade loop. Once word spread among the local clans, this abuse stopped. The Outpost, they learned, was a place in which to conduct serious trade.

The tripartite clan that was now leaving carried between them several parcels sealed in the ubiquitous, biodegradable plastic wrap that was used to package all trade goods. As he watched them depart, Stefan directed the room's air purifier to grade up a notch. Allawout body odor was no more pleasing than their appearance. In a few minutes the atmospheric scrubber would have removed the last lingering odiferous traces of the clan's visit.

Pervasatha waited for the cheerful, noisily bubbling family to exit before coming in. Despite his special cooling gear, he was sweating profusely. A number of visiting supervisors and scientists felt that would have been a better name for the planet: Sweating Profusely. It was certainly more descriptive than Irelis IV.

"Got something for you, Stef." Perv, as his friends and co-workers called him, leaned one elbow down on the counter. The corners of his mouth twitched. He seemed to be striving hard to repress a grin.

"Not another carved Ohrus tooth." Stefan eyed the other young man warily. "They're pretty, but we've already got a boxful."

"Nope. Better than that." The grin escaped its bounds. Perv pointed to the door. "Enter! Come inside."

A native slid slowly inward on the familiar, disgusting trail of lubricating gunk. Behind it, the floor did its best to clean up after the visitor. Unfeeling mechanical though it was, Stefan still felt sorry for the autocleaner. Unlike the rest of them, it could never look forward to a day off. Not on Irelis.

Perv's grin was wider than ever. "You remember that directive? Not last week's—the one before. Page twelve. 'All company Outposts must strive where possible to encourage local life forms to participate in the ongoing activities of a given station, with regard to maintaining and enhancing benign relations between the human and native populations.'"

"Yeah." Stefan was immediately on guard. "I remember it. So what?" He slapped at his forehead, smashing something small, irritating, and resistant to the day's cocktail of insecticides that he had liberally applied earlier.

Perv gestured grandly at the newcomer, who was gazing around at the interior of the station with eyes that were even wider than normal. "Meet your new native assistant!"

Stefan blanched, recovered when he thought it was a joke, eyed his friend in disbelief when it began to sink it that it was not. "Don't try to be funny, Perv. It's too hot today."

"And it'll be too hot tomorrow, and the day after that, and the one after that also. But this blob of gray goo is still your new assistant. Morey says so."

"Screw Morey!" As if the native was not present, Stefan gestured in its direction. "We don't have indigenous assistants. No local works inside the Outpost."

"We do now," Perv shot back. "They do now."

The other man's eyes narrowed. "Then where's *your* assistant?"

"Regulations say that, at this point in the Outpost's development, we only need one. She's it. She's yours." His smile flattened. "Lack of seniority says so."

"'She?'" A dubious Stefan studied the lumpish native, who continued to ignore the two young humans as she gawked at the interior of the trading room. "I thought the biologists hadn't figured out how to sex them yet."

Perv stood away from the counter. "Far as I know, they haven't. But that's the classification I've been given." He winked and turned to go. "I'll leave you two alone now."

The other man gestured wildly. "Hey, wait a minute! What am I supposed to do with this—with 'her'?"

Perv kept walking. "Not my concern. Morey says she's your new assistant. Get her to assist. Me, I've got work to do on the bromide concentrator or the delay'll go down on my record." He exited at a brisk clip, not looking back.

Stefan was once again alone in the room. Well, not quite.

Maybe if he ignored the native, it would go away. Sitting back down, he muttered the "unpause" command and resumed watching the word play he had been engrossed in prior to the trading clan's arrival. Images danced in the air half a meter in front of his eyes. After a while, he became aware that he was not alone. As was often the case, it was the smell that tipped him off.

Advancing silently on its sheet of motive slime, the Allawout had sidled up as close behind him as it dared, and was dutifully gazing up at images whose origin, meaning, and purpose must be as alien to it as tooth gel.

Nostrils flexing in revulsion, he looked over his shoulder and down at the creature. Morey had declared it was his new assistant. Until he could make the notoriously gruff Outpost administrator who supervised all the young apprentices like himself see reason, Stefan realized with a sinking feeling that he was probably stuck with the creature. But fortunately, he told himself, not to it. If he abused it physically, there could be trouble. Members of the station's scientific contingent, who infrequently mixed with the much younger and less experienced team of trader apprentices, would report him. His advancement up the company ladder would be questioned, and he might even be dropped down a rating or two. That could not be allowed to happen. Not after the horrid half year he had already been forced to put in on Irelis.

Swallowing his distaste, he asked in terranglo, "Do you have a name?"

The dumpy alien quivered revoltingly, as if trying to slough off its skin. Flesh-protecting mucus oozed from pores and slid down its sides. "I am chosen Uluk."

At least it could talk a little, the apprentice reflected. Come to think of it, the staff would not have selected one to work inside the station, with humans, unless it had acquired at least some facility with the language of the visitors. Then something happened that completely broke his train of thought.

Raising a tentacle, the Allawout pointed at the hovering word play image and said, "Pretty—what means it?"

It was the first time in nearly six months that Stefan had heard a local ask a question not directly related to trading. Minimal fluency he had expected: intellectual curiosity, if such it could be called, was something new. Without pausing to wonder why he was bothering to reply, he struggled to explain something of the subtle nature of a word play.

She did not understand. That was not surprising. Had she comprehended even his childishly simple explanation, he would immediately have passed her along to the scientific staff as an exemplar of Allawout acumen. On the indigenous scale of intelligence she doubtless qualified as quite bright. About at the level of a human eight-year old, only without any book learning to draw upon. It was unlikely she would grow any smarter.

But as the months progressed, she did. Or at least, her vocabulary increased. Struggling with the most fundamental concepts, she did everything he asked of her, from laboriously dragging trade goods into the back chamber to be sorted, catalogued, pre-priced, and packaged for shipment off-world; to making suggestions to visiting locals about what goods the strange dry-skin folk preferred and would pay well for.

It was funny to see how the other natives deferred to her. Even mature males, muscular of tentacle and sharp of eye, seemed to shrink slightly in her presence. For a wild moment he thought she might be some kind of local equivalent of royalty, much as the notion of an

Allawout princess seemed a contradiction in terms. Belleau Lormantz, one of the xenologists, assured him that could not be the case.

"In the nearly twenty years there has been a human presence on Irelis, no evidence has surfaced of any level of government above that of the extended family or clan. They haven't even achieved the tribal level yet. They're just starting to emerge from the hunter-gatherer stage." Belleau had a nice voice, Stefan mused. About the nicest voice on Irelis. And unlike most of the scientists, she was nearly the same age as he was.

They were sitting together on one of the elevated walkways built atop balumina pilings that had been driven down through water and muck into the reluctant bedrock far below. Redder than that of his homeworld, Irelis's sun was setting behind tall strands of red and yellow fiberthrush, the light peeking through the fronds to illuminate the station's sealed, welded-together, prefabricated modules. Belleau was almost as reflective as the metal walls, he decided.

A voice sounded behind them, plaintive yet insistent. "Stef-han, what should I do with kaja bowls just buying today?"

He looked around irritably. "They go in the back, on the bottom shelves on the right-hand side. You know that, Uluk!"

Her tone did not change, and she had no expression to alter. "Yes, Stef-han. I will make it so." It took her several minutes to slip-slide back inside.

He returned to contemplating the sunset, the violet underside of the evening cumulus filling his head with thoughts that did not belong in as unpleasant a place as the Outpost.

"I hear that you're leaving the station."

She nodded. "Sabbatical. On Rhenoull V. To consolidate my reports, put some into book form, give lectures—that sort of thing. I think I'll be back, to start in on my advanced work. There's a lot about these creatures we still don't know."

"Is there that much more to learn?" When she did not comment, he added, "How do I know you're coming back, Belle?"

"Because I say so. Because my work is here."

He peered deep into her eyes. Perspiration glistened like pale pearls on her forehead and cheeks. She was wet, tired, unkempt, and beautiful. "Is that the only reason?"

She turned away from him, seeking surcease in the sunset. "I'm not sure—yet," she replied candidly. "I like you, Stefan. I like you a lot. But I'm so deep into my work that much of the time I feel like I'm drowning."

"Drown in me," he told her with more intensity than he intended.

Her hand slipped sideways to cover his. "Maybe when I come back," she told him frankly. "When I have more confidence in my own future. Then, maybe—we'll see. You're a little young for me, Stefan."

"I'm not that young." When he reached for her, she leaned away, laughing affectionately. "No, not now. As sweaty as we are, if we hold each other too tightly, we're liable to slip right past each other and into the water."

He laughed too, and settled for squeezing her hand while waiting for the alien sun to finish its day's work.

He sweated out another six months, her absence made all the more frustrating by his having to deal with Uluk. Just when it seemed she was acquiring some real skill, she would do something supremely stupid. He was forced to reprimand her, sigh in exasperation, and explain the procedure all over again. She would listen patiently, indicate understanding, go along fine for a while, and eventually repeat the same mistake. Something about the Allawout seemed to render them incapable of retaining any pattern of information for more than a few weeks at a time. It was as if the entire species was afflicted with attention span deficit disorder. To make matters worse, he had to endure the endless jokes and gags the rest of the staff enjoyed at his expense. His only compensation was the occasional reluctant, approving grunt from Administrator Morey, who recognized the strain his most junior underling was operating under. That, plus praise from the scientific staff. The behaviorists in particular would seek him out to query him interminably about his conversations with the Allawout.

"Look," he would object in exasperation, "we don't have 'conversations.' I give the thing orders, and she carries them out. Except when she forgets what to do, which is all the time, and I have to explain them all over again. Slowly and repeatedly, in the simplest terms possible."

"But within those constraints," a much older xenologist had pressed him, "the native in question *is* capable of performing the complex tasks she is assigned by you."

"Sure," he joked, "if you can call stacking carvings and sorting voull horns 'complex.' Anything that involves actually thinking I have to guide and help her with. Initiative doesn't exist among the Alla-wout. Except where it concerns food and shelter, I personally don't think they have any understanding of the concept."

"But the other locals obviously respect her deeply." The scientist had been persistent.

"Sure!" Stefan agreed. "She's big stuff because she has a job in the House-of-Wonders-That-Stands-in-Water, and speaks freely to the visitors from the cloud rafts. I suppose," he conceded, "that gives her some kind of rank, or status, that places her a notch above her fellow weed munchers."

A few such carefully chosen comments were usually sufficient to send the behaviorists on their contemplative way, muttering to themselves. One nice thing about Stefan's assistant, as far as Morey was concerned, was that the native never questioned her status. She accepted payment in trade goods, never asked for a change in the amount or kind of remuneration, worked silently and steadily, and was a real help in communicating the wants of the human traders to the indigenes who arrived to partake of the marvels to be had at the station. She slept in an old concentrate barrel Perv had welded to one of the balumina stilts, just above the waterline. Each morning she would ooze out, drop into the water to clean herself, and then slide up the ramp that had been erected to provide her kind with easy access to the station. With their strong tentacles they could easily climb a ladder, but that would not allow them to bring goods into or take them out of the Outpost. Stefan had despaired of ever seeing Belleau again. Then one day, slightly less than a month before his tour was up and he was due to be promoted off-world, suddenly she was there, having arrived without notice on the monthly shuttle. They did not exactly fall into one another's arms—not with Customs officials and everyone else watching. But their glances met, spoke, and smiled. Certain decisions were arrived at without the use of words.

"I told you I'd come back," she whispered to him later that morning.

"To finish your work?" He left the question hanging, too fearful to add the anxious corollary he was burning to ask.

"To do that, yes—and perhaps," she added mischievously, "to attend to other matters."

"I'm done here in a few weeks." They were standing in the Outpost, its familiar overheated surroundings for once the equal and not the excess of what he was feeling inside. "The Company has offered me my choice of positions. On civilized worlds, at a higher salary. I have a lot of flexibility."

"Hmm. That does open certain possibilities, doesn't it? For example, I've taken a lectureship on Mathewson III."

He managed to maintain an even tone. "There are two Company operations on Mathewson. Big ones."

She nodded thoughtfully. Then she leaned forward, kissed him once, adequately, and almost ran from the room. He remained behind, dazed and relieved and overflowing with contentment.

Behind him, an odor preceded a query. "Stef-han is happy?"

His expression fell. The wondrous contentment rushed away like water through the bottom of a broken jar. Work called.

"Yes, Uluk. Stefan happy. Stefan go away soon."

"Go away?" Crescent pupils swam within disc-like eyes. "Why Stefan go away?"

"It's time to go," he muttered irritably. "All sky folk eventually go from Irelis. Go back to home." At her uncomprehending silence he added, "Back to own raft."

She appeared to consider this. "Outpost not Stef-han's raft?"

"No, dammit. Don't you have something to do?"

"Yes. I forget."

Lifting his eyes heavenward, he moved to check the duty scan for the day. But nothing, not even Allawout doltishness, could entirely mitigate the joy Belle's arrival and greeting had engendered.

The next several weeks passed in a haze that was more a consequence of his re-establishing his relationship with Belleau than of the heavy atmosphere. They spoke of her science and his business, and how the two might complement one another on a world like Mathewson III. When it was clear that the positives outweighed the negatives, their delight was mutual. They were both very practical people.

When it was time to go, to finally leave behind Irelis and its miasmatic swamps and lugubrious atmosphere and multifarious stinks and smells, it was almost an anticlimax. Morey was there to see them both off and to wish them well, the taciturn old Company man unable to look his former employee in the face for fear of giving way to an actual smile. Pervasatha was long gone, having been promoted ahead of Stefan, but several others among the scientific and commercial community who had established friendships with the personable young trader on his way up turned out to see him and his lady off.

They were waiting for the skimmer that would ferry them out to the distant shuttle site, an artificial island built out in the middle of a voluminous lake, when it occurred to Stefan that something was missing. A certain stench....

"Funny," he mused aloud, "I thought she'd come to say good-bye."

"'She?'" Belleau's querulous tone mimicked one he himself had used some time ago.

"My indigenous assistant. An Allawout nominated Uluk. You met her. Or at least, you encountered her."

"Oh yes, of course. I only saw her a couple of times. She was usually working in the rear storeroom whenever I came into the Outpost."

He found himself searching the station's walkways, then the lethargic muck beneath. "I thought she'd be here." He shrugged. "Oh well. No matter. She probably forgot." Turning back to Belleau, he smiled lovingly. "After a year here I don't know how I'll cope with a normal, Earth-type climate."

"I give you about two days to become fully acclimated," she replied teasingly.

Henderson came huffing and puffing down the walkway. Reaching out, the panting behaviorist caught his breath as he shook first the trader's hand, then Belleau's. "Wanted to wish luck to you both. I'm sure you won't need it."

Stefan nodded his thanks. "Say, you haven't by any chance seen Uluk around today?"

"Your indigene assistant?" Henderson's expression fell. "Oh. I thought you knew. They found her yesterday, about half a kilometer from the station. On Islet Twelve. Dead. Self-inflicted killing wound, the biologists tell me. Sorry."

Something very strange congealed in the trader's gut. But it went away quickly. "That's too bad. I wonder what happened."

Henderson cast a quick glance in Belleau's direction before replying. She was a fellow scientist, after all, and the incident was an interesting comment on indigenous behavioral patterns.

"You really didn't know, did you? No, you wouldn't, being always focused on commerce, and trade balances, and the like. The Allawout's focus is on extended family groupings, or clans. Alpha males and females, Beta juniors, and so on. Didn't you ever notice that Uluk was never seen interacting with a family grouping?"

Stefan shrugged indifferently. "You're right. I never thought about it. She lived alone at the station. That was her choice. Morey, myself, everyone else—we all thought that was her choice."

"Oh, it was, it was," Henderson hastened to assure him. "I spoke to her several times, you know. My work." He added almost apologetically. "You didn't know that she was focused on you?"

The trader eyed the behaviorist uncertainly. "On me? Why would I ever notice something like that?"

Belleau's response was more understanding. "Are you saying that this Uluk individual chose to imprint on Stefan in lieu of a normal Allawout extended family grouping?"

"The two of them worked together. Almost every day." Henderson looked contrite. "I thought surely you would have sensed something, Stefan, or I would have mentioned something about it to you. It makes for a very interesting case history. In the absence of any other extended family members, it's not uncommon for the Allawout to terminate themselves instead of attempting to impose themselves on another family or clan."

"C'mon, Tom!" Even as he remonstrated with the behaviorist, Stefan found himself scanning the vegetation of the distant, fetid swampland. He remembered how Uluk had hovered about him, lingering in his vicinity even when work was done; watching him operate the projector and the viewers; asking questions to which he was sure she already knew the answers. How she was always there waiting for him in the mornings, and leaving reluctantly when it was time to retire to her barrel.

"It's not unprecedented." The behaviorist was eying his departing acquaintance regretfully. "The Allawout don't show physical affection. It would hardly have been appropriate in this instance anyway."

"You mean," Belleau ventured, "what happened was akin to a dog pining away for its master?"

"Well, hardly." Henderson drew himself up slightly. "The Allawout may be a little slow on the uptake, but they're far from unaware."

He turned back to the now silent, staring trader. "It's not your fault, you know. Happens all the time with these clans. Self-termination is a well-documented means of controlling the population and maintaining the available food supply."

"Oh, I know." Stefan seemed to shake himself. "It's too bad. She was nice enough—except for the smell. I can't help it if she was somehow attracted to one of the sky people. To me." The oddest sensation was spreading through him. It made him angry, but try as he might, he found he could not suppress it.

"'Attracted?'" Henderson peered at him a little harder. "You really *didn't* notice anything, did you? Uluk wasn't attracted to you. We spoke about many such things, and I remember quite clearly that she told me once she thought you were the ugliest living thing she had ever set eyes upon. That's why she stayed at the Outpost so long, and close to you." Wiping his eyes, the behaviorist blinked back the unforgiving rays of the setting violet sun.

"She felt sorry for you."

4

Chilling

My third original novel was a book called Icerigger. *It's June here in Arizona as I write this, and as I recall, it was a hot time in Santa Monica, California, when I wrote that.* Icerigger *was my first book-length attempt at creating an alien world and while it was steamy outside my apartment, I was able to cool down by imagining the frozen world of Tran-Ky-Ky and its diverse well-adapted denizens.*

As time and other stories came to pass and readers told me how much they enjoyed that world and its ecology, I eventually decided to write a sequel. That became Mission to Moulokin. *More years gone by, more stories scribed, and I thought there might still be tale to be told that would wrap up the adventures of the principle characters in the first two novels. Hence,* The Deluge Drivers.

Thus I was done with Tran-ky-ky and its blade-mounted natives and ice-dwelling fauna. Until a request came in for a story to be included in an on-line only magazine. Maybe it was a hot day: I don't remember. But today is, and that makes it more agreeable still to be … chilling.

"YOU STUPID IDIOT, you've killed us!"

Arik looked over at his new wife. "I love you, too."

They sat on opposite sides of the cave. It was not much of a cave. At its highest the ceiling barely allowed him enough room to stand, and it could not have been more than six or seven meters wide. But compared to the frozen howling wilderness outside it might as well have been the Garden of Eden. Strange fungal growths carpeted the surface of the interior with a subdued cerulean radiance while coiled flowerless scrubs no higher than a man's knee clustered as close to the bubbling central pool as possible. Twitching yellow-brown tendrils hung from the ceiling, reaching toward the geothermal heat. While individual specimens occasionally emitted a soft whistle, without pulling one free from its perch and taking it apart Arik was unable to tell if they were plant or animal. Jen refused to touch them.

One of several thermal springs that dotted the tiny island on which the cave was located, the hot pool was what was keeping the two humans as well as the exotic flora alive. While certain specialized growths like pika-pina and the much larger pika-pedan flourished out on the bare frozen oceans of Tran-ky-ky, rarer flora like the orange fiesin were restricted to locales where the ice world's internal heat reached the surface. The cloud of steam generated by one such thermal vent was what had initially drawn him and Jen to the island. A sister spring was also the cause of their present predicament.

Sitting back against the wall of the cave with his knees drawn up to his chest and his bare hands extended toward the life-preserving warmth of the bubbling spring, Arik reflected that their present desperate situation was not wholly his fault. The Tran who had rented them the small native iceboat should have provided more detailed advice about the possible dangers to be encountered out on the frozen ocean. Or perhaps the native had done so and Arik's translator had failed to interpret everything correctly. The latter was not an impossibility. Not on a world that had only recently applied for associate Commonwealth membership, where the sale and use of advanced technology was still forbidden to the local sentients, and where along with so much else the study of the strongly guttural native language was still in its infancy.

Jen looked across at him. Having slipped out of the cheap daysuit, she was sitting nearly naked next to the pool. She would gladly have immersed herself in it if not for the fact that even at its edges the surface temperature was close to boiling.

Some choice they had, he mused. Poach in the pool inside the cave or freeze in the air outside it.

"We're not dead yet." He tried to reassure her.

"Might as well be." She was chewing on a fingernail. Because of the hot spring the air inside the cave was warm enough for them to remove their protective daysuits. Outside—outside was another matter entirely. Another world, in every sense of the word. Tran-ky-ky's vast oceans were frozen solid to varying but usually considerable depths, exposed earth crackled and snapped beneath one's boots, a gust of wind sent sharp pain racing through unprotected eyes, and on a more intimate note the moisture in a person's nose caused the hairs to freeze almost instantly on contact with the air.

They had arrived as passengers on a wide-ranging interstellar transport, intending to visit this new outpost of the Commonwealth only for the couple of days the KK-drive craft spent off-loading cargo. When it re-entered space plus on its way to the next system, they would go with it. It was a journey as unorthodox as it was costly. Interstellar travel was too expensive and time-consuming to allow people to journey lazily from system to system. Citizens traveled from point to point with very definite destinations in mind.

The atypical post-marriage journey was a present from their respective families, each of whom happened to be quite wealthy. All the credit in the Commonwealth, however, had not prevented the new couple's rented iceboat from sinking.

How was he to have known that a subsurface fumarole had melted and weakened the ice close to the island where they had decided to come ashore? Or that anything called a "boat" would promptly sink when exposed to open water? In retrospect, of course, it all made perfect if disheartening sense. Designed to skim across the frozen sea on runners chiseled from solid marble-like stone, the craft had been built to skate, not to float. Why would anyone on Tran-ky-ky build something capable of floating when there was no open water for it to float upon? It was solid ice everywhere, solid ice all the time. Even if the material of which the iceboat had been fashioned had been sufficiently buoyant, the craft still would have been dragged down by the weight of its stone runners.

They had set out for the day trip from the outpost of Brass Monkey. Located not far north of the planetary Equator, it was the headquarters of the sole human settlement on the planet. Journey further north, they had been told, and the climate made getting around difficult for even those humans equipped with modern arctic gear. Far to the east lay the enormous volcano whose Tran name translated as The-Place-Where-the-Earth's-Blood-Burns. According to the small but steadily expanding information file on Tran-ky-ky, between the volcano and the mountainous lands of Arsudun where Brass Monkey was located lay a multitude of small islands. Some of these were home to distinctive biological environments abounding with endemic species, many of which had yet to be identified and scientifically described. The island on which they currently found themselves marooned was one such outpost of unique indigenous biological diversity.

He estimated that it was just past noon local time. He had to estimate because their communicators had gone down with the iceboat. He chose not to try and guess the temperature outside the cave. When they had arrived at the island his communicator had declared that the temperature was minus twenty-one centigrade with a wind chill double, possibly triple that. Cold enough to kill. Tonight it would drop to that point. Tomorrow morning—tomorrow it might not matter. Like everything else they had brought with them, their self-heating meals had gone down with the iceboat. Having been raised in a privileged family where only the quality and never the quantity of the food he had eaten had ever been in question he had no idea how long a person could survive sans nourishment. Even in the semi-protected environment of the cave.

Of course, if the spring that supplied the hot pool turned out to be inconsistent and chose to stop bubbling for awhile, the heat it provided would be quickly sucked from the small cavern. They would die swiftly and without having to worry about food.

"'Visit some of the Commonwealth's most exotic locations before we settle down on Earth,' you said. 'Experience the hard-to-see worlds while we're still young enough to do so in comfort,' you said."

Muttering under her breath, Jen moved her feet closer to the bubbling pool. She wished she could ease her legs into the boiling water. Arik felt it was too risky. Reluctantly, she agreed with him. If the temperature rose suddenly she ran a real risk of being scalded. She had to settle for scooping her hands quickly in and out of the water and splashing her face and body.

"I didn't hear any violent objections from you when the trip was being organized," he shot back.

"I had this, in retrospect, unreasonable expectation that you might know what you were doing." One hand gestured in the direction of the cave opening. Outside, the wind sang sub-zero. "You could have at least had the sense to bring along our gear pack when we got off the boat."

Said gear pack, which held all their food, drinks, chemical reaction space heater, and most important of all any means of communicating with civilization, had gone down with the iceboat when it had fallen through the thin pane of ice that had been undermined by the hidden fumarole. At least they had water, though they dared not drink directly from the effervescent pool. It reeked of sulfur and other minerals. For all they knew, it was rich in dissolved arsenic. So they grabbed snow from outside the cave entrance and held it in their hands just above the hot mineral water until it melted.

They did not even have a cup, he reflected morosely.

"I didn't see *you* carrying anything off the boat when we came ashore." His tone was accusing.

"I didn't think we'd be here more than ten or fifteen minutes," she countered unhappily. "Half an hour at most."

He saw no point in arguing further. Mutual accusations accomplished nothing. Half an hour maximum. That had been the plan. It was no one's fault, certainly not his, that the sub-heated ice had given way beneath the modest weight of their iceboat. If they had been traveling airborne, now, in a proper skimmer ... But the use of such advanced technology outside the boundaries of the station was forbidden.

He'd had no trouble navigating the simple single-sail iceboat. An experienced open-water sailor, he had found the native rigging not so very different from that of a small recreational sailing vessel back home. The native Tran had been using multiple permutations of such craft for centuries. He and Jen had even had the opportunity to take a tour of its most recent elaboration, the massive icerigger *Slanderscree* that had been tied up in the harbor.

"Someone will find us," he assured her more gently. "We were supposed to have been back late yesterday afternoon. The native who rented us the iceboat will have informed the proper authorities."

Using spread fingers, she brushed out her shoulder-length blonde hair. Rich and beautiful, he thought as he looked at her. If someone did not find them today, by tomorrow she might be rich and dead. She would certainly make the more attractive corpse of the two.

"It's one thing for the people at the station to be informed that we're missing," she muttered unhappily. "It's another for someone to find us."

Rising, he walked around the small pool and sat down close to her. Her anger had moderated enough so that this time she did not object. "Emergency position locators are designed to keep operating under severe conditions. Even submerged in ice water the one on the iceboat could still be functioning."

"Unless harsh chemicals from the hot vent corroded it as soon as it sank."

Now why did she have to go and point that out, he asked himself? If their personal communicators and the locator that had been on the iceboat had failed, then no one would know where they were. While they had not traveled all that many kilometers from Brass Monkey, they had not sailed in a straight line. As tourists, they had taken their time and wandered around. They would be difficult to track even if the original angle of their departure had been observed and noted.

Unlike Jen, he had stayed dressed. Looking down, he checked the weather seals at wrists and ankles. The daysuit was designed to keep an individual comfortable while outside even in Tran-ky-ky's climate. But the chemicals in the fabric that combined to generate heat when the suit was put on were intended to last no more than a couple of days. In contrast, a fully-powered cold climate survival suit of the type worn by the scientists at the outpost would use a combination of solar, chemical, cell, and the body's own internal heat to keep a traveler warm indefinitely.

But why would anyone need one of the bulkier, more expensive survival suits just to go out for a mid-day jaunt? A simpler, cheaper, disposable daysuit would serve perfectly well.

For a day or two.

He started to shiver. "We're going to have to risk bathing in a shallow part of the pool. Near the far edge." He nodded. "The water temperature is lower there."

"Yeah. For the moment and barring any tectonic surprises." Her expression twisted. "But sure, let's risk that. You go first."

"We'll step in together." He revised his suggestion.

"Not a chance, Arik. If you suddenly start to cook, I need to be able to pull you out. And vice versa when it's my turn." She eyed him evenly. "And don't say anything to me about how romantic a mutual dip would be. I'm not in the mood."

Their present situation was not, he decided, what was generally meant when a relationship was described as blowing hot and cold. He edged over until he was sitting up against her. His left arm went around her shoulder.

"Look, I'm sorry, okay? The information file on this world said the oceans here never melt. Nothing was said about keeping an eye out for liquid water in the vicinity of subterranean thermal activity." He hugged her. This time she leaned into him instead of away, which was encouraging. Or maybe she was just looking for a little extra warmth.

"We're going to die," she reiterated glumly. "Married less than two months and I'm going to die."

"Someone will find us. They must have started searching this morning, even in this weather, and …"

As if in direct response to his encouraging words a shape appeared outside the entrance to the cave. Springing to his feet and bending over to avoid bumping into the low ceiling, he started excitedly forward.

"See, I told you!" he called back to the equally excited Jen. "Everything'll be all right now. Hey!" Slipping his gloves back on and resealing them to the wrists of the daysuit he started forward while waving his hands. "Hey, we're in here! We're okay!" Behind him, Jen was hastily climbing into her own suit.

The shape stopped and turned to look at him. It was a big man. No, he quickly corrected himself, it was bigger than a man. Its ventral side narrowed to a sharp V-shape where bone had fused to form a solid keel. A pair of legs on either side resembled hairy flippers that terminated in downward-curving twin spikes. There was no neck. Jutting out from the stout cylindrical body, the tapering head terminated in a wide, flat mouth suitable for snatching things off the ice. The jaws were filled with curved, hook-like teeth that pointed in all directions, designed to impale and hold squirming, fast-moving prey. Protected by double transparent eyelids, both pale green eyes focused avidly on Arik.

Behind him Jen inhaled sharply. Neither of them had any idea what the creature was. They did not remember it from the very limited guidebook. Evolved to live and thrive on open, bare ice, Tran-ky-ky's fauna was as exotic as its flora. From the look of it, this particular carnivore probably traveled by lying on its skate-like keel bone and pulling itself forward by jamming its cramponish flipper-spikes into the ice. That it could also drag itself forward on solid ground was self-evident from the way it now began to pull itself into the cave. It was likely, Arik decided as he retreated, that the menacing beast was not nearly as agile on land as it was out on the open ice.

It was, however, plenty big enough to completely block the only exit.

As it shoved its head further into the cave opening it emitted a deep, reverberant moan that sounded more like the cry of something giving birth subsequent to a delayed pregnancy than it did a predatory challenge.

"Do something!" Jen yelled as she hurriedly resealed her gloves.

Keeping one eye on the lurching, advancing predator, Arik searched the cave as he continued to back up. They had no weapons. What would anyone need with weapons on a one-day sight-seeing trip? It was a moot regret. Even if they had brought one along it would have gone down on the iceboat with the rest of their equipment.

Jen picked up a rock and threw it. It produced a reverberant *thunk* as it struck the intruder, the same kind of dull sound she had heard when she had once been forced to slap an over-amorous dolphin.

The stone bounced off the carnivore exactly as if it had hit a hunk of solid rubber. Hacking up another eager moan, the creature continued to drag itself deeper into the cave. Its bulk scoured gravel and rock dust from the walls. There was no possible way they could get around it.

"Keep the pool between it and us!" Arik had retreated to join Jen and take her hand. He squeezed it firmly and she replied in kind. "It's adapted to permanent cold, so it might avoid the hot water. If it comes at us from the left, we go right. If it comes right, we make a run for it around the other side of the pool."

"Great," she commented dryly. "Then what?"

Then—they would be outside, he realized. In their failing daysuits.

Could the creature run them down? And if so, would it start to consume them before they froze and died?

Arching back its head, the intruder bellowed sharply. It was a completely different sound from the enthusiastic moaning it had been emitting thus far. The source of the cry soon became apparent.

First one spear, then a second, then two more struck the animal from behind, the sharp points driving deeply into the thickly-insulated flesh. As the beleaguered creature roared and bellowed in pain it rocked back and forth against the walls of the cave. Stone shards and ice crystals broke loose. The creature's dying cacophony was awful to hear. A dust cloud of pulverized rock filled the cavity that housed the pool, causing both humans to break out coughing.

It took twenty minutes for the embattled carnivore to die. Then all was silent except for the hot spring's persistent gurgling and the lonesome whine of the wind outside.

Waving dust away from his face, Arik advanced cautiously toward the exit. Something he could not see was pulling the now deceased beast backwards and out of the cave. He strained for a better look.

"It's okay," he told Jen. "I can count spears sticking out of it." His heart leaped. "It has to be the natives. We're saved!"

There were half a dozen of them; tall, densely furred, dressed in heavy, well-made clothing fashioned of wind-breaking leathers and the cured skins of lesser fauna. Large furry ears stuck out from the sides of their heads while oval cat-like eyes gazed into the wind from behind double lids. Two of them boasted beards that blended without a break into the fur that covered their elongated faces. The membranous *dan* that formed wind-catching wings hung limp from wrists to waists.

Sharp knives emerged from scabbards and flashed in the brilliant sunlight as they began to cut up the dead carnivore. Sunlight glinted off the extended, backward curving claws on their feet. Called *chiv*, these remarkable evolutionary adaptations allowed the Tran to skate on their bare feet across the endless expanses of ice.

Arik was so relieved to see them that when he hurried outside he did not even bother to snap down his protective face shield. "Hello, hello! O'Morion, are we glad to see you! We've been stuck here for ..."

The fist that struck him was as unyielding as it was unexpected. When his momentarily blurred vision cleared again it was to reveal two of the natives standing over him, swords drawn. Piercing eyes that were feline yet alien bored into his own. He ignored the chill that was creeping over his face.

"Hey, what's the idea? What …?" He started to rise.

One of the Tran put a foot on his chest and shoved. Gently, so that the triple razor-sharp chiv on the bottom of his foot would not slice into the human's daysuit. The pair of armed locals began chattering animatedly among themselves. Though Arik knew nothing of the local language, the tone of the natives' conversation did not strike him as cordial.

"Arik!"

Looking to his right he saw that two more of them were dragging Jen out of the cave. She'd had the foresight to flip down her face shield. Behind her the remaining pair of Tran continued to work on the carcass of the dead predator.

"Keep calm!" He struggled to remember what he had read of this world. Despite its recent application for associate Commonwealth membership, many of the natives of Tran-ky-ky lived in a semi-feudal society. It was said that there still remained a number to be convinced of the benefits of Commonwealth membership. Not all had voted in favor of it.

Could it be, he found himself thinking uneasily, that those who had landed on the island might just possibly fall into the latter social group?

With only primitive blades at their disposal two of them were rapidly reducing the remains of the dead carnivore to chops, steaks, and the equivalent of local prime cuts. Steam rose from the gaping, disemboweled corpse. Would he and Jen be next?

After cleaning his blade in the snow and then wiping it dry against his gray jerkin, the tallest Tran scabbarded it and walked over to gaze down at the humans. As the alien approached, Jen edged sideways until she was standing behind her new husband. They eyed the natives warily. After inspecting them both, the knife wielder focused yellow eyes on Arik. At a gesture, the Tran with a foot on the human's chest stepped back and allowed him to stand.

"I hight Signur Draz-hode." Though he sounded as if he was talking with a mouthful of gravel, the Tran's terranglo was quite intelligible. With a clawed hand he indicated his companions. As he raised his arm, his right dan unfurled like a translucent cape. "We are kurgals of the Virin Clan." Leaning forward, he studied the two humans more closely. "Though you have not the look of invaders, that does not absolve you."

"Invaders?" Behind her face shield, Jen blinked. "We're not invaders."

"We're tourists," Arik added helpfully.

"'Tourists'?" The Virin Signur Draz-hode's command of terranglo was not perfect.

"Visitors," Jen explained. "Sightseers. Casual travelers who are here for only a day to see some of your unique world. To enjoy its ice oceans and snow-covered mountains, its plant and animal life." Maintaining a smile, she nodded in the direction of the gutted, steaming carcass nearby. "Like that."

Straightening, Draz-hode turned into the wind to eye the corpse. Fully adapted to the unrelenting climate, he needed no face shield. "A sodj? There is nothing unique about a sodj. Even in taste it is ordinary. But it was the best we could find on this hunting journey." He looked back at her. "Until now."

"Until ...?" She swallowed hard. "You're—you're going to eat us?"

It took a moment for the Tran to dissolve the human words in his mind. When understanding finally came, he howled with laughter. At least, Arik assumed it was laughter. It certainly was a howl. When the Tran translated for his hunting companions, they promptly mimicked his vocalization. To Arik it sounded like a chorus of tenors warming up for a concert by engaging in a coughing contest.

Eventually Draz-hode recovered sufficiently to regard the female human once more. "We might—later. For now, we have the sodj. You are invaders. You come to our world and turn everything upside town. You insist we make a government not of peoples and clans but of all mixed together without regard to history or honor. You trample tradition under your soft, chiv-less feet!"

"*We* don't," Jen argued as forcefully as she dared. "We don't trample anything. We're not politicians. We're just tourists."

"You'll be better off as citizens of the Commonwealth," Arik could not resist saying. "You'll have modern conveniences, medicine, technology, exposure to the arts and culture of other races ..."

Draz-hode interrupted him roughly. "Who asked for the things of which you speak? Not I. Not the Virin. Yet your allies and our traditional enemies try to force them upon us. So be it. The Virin can adapt to new circumstances without foregoing the old. You wish to see some of our 'unique' world? You will be given that opportunity." He added something in the guttural yet attractive local tongue.

His companions came forward. Using cord woven from strips of pika-pedan they secured the prisoners' arms behind their backs. One of the natives automatically started to furl the dan he expected to see running from Arik's waist up to his arm before remembering that humans did not possess the tough membrane that allowed the Tran to speed across the ice with only the wind at their backs to propel them.

"What are you going to do with us?" a worried Arik asked their captor.

Draz-hode did not hesitate. "Ransom. It is an old and venerable custom among our kind. We will find out if it operates similarly among your people." He exposed sharp teeth. "Call it cultural exchange."

"We've traveled here on our own," Jen put in. "It would take a long time to work out the details of such a trade."

Walking up to the female human, Draz-hode bent forward so that his face was close to hers. For a second time, he showed his teeth. "In that eventuality we will find out how you taste. If it turns out that you are not worth money, you will still be valuable as food."

As he and Jen were marched down the uneven slope toward the hunters' waiting iceboat Arik noted that their captors did not bind their legs. There was no need. If they did somehow manage to escape they could not possibly walk all the way back to Brass Monkey. They could not walk, period. Unlike the Tran whose razor-sharp chiv protruded from the undersides of their feet, the boots he and Jen were wearing would find them slipping and sliding all over the ice if they tried to hike more than a few meters.

Their captor's iceboat was considerably bigger than his and Jen's day rental. It had a higher mast, a crude bowsprit equipped with a foresheet, a pika-pedan railing, and a much larger central cabin. Essentially an arrowhead-shaped raft mounted on runners of cut and polished stone, it also featured a pointed stern to which a fourth runner was attached. Unlike the three forward runners that were fixed in position, the one aft was attached to a tiller that served to steer the craft.

With proportionately longer arms than a human, the lean and muscular virin had no trouble hauling their prisoners up onto the open raft. Once all were aboard, the single square sail was let out. As soon as the boat cleared the lee of the island and encountered a steady breeze it began to rapidly pick up speed.

"Don't worry," Arik whispered to his new wife. "One of the search parties will find us."

She glared moodily back at him. "First, you're assuming there are search parties out looking for us. Second, you're assuming at least one of them will have some idea where to look. Third, at the speed we're making now we'll soon be far from any hypothetical area where any hypothetical search party might choose to hypothetically search. Fourth, you're an idiot."

Lying on his side on the rough-hewn deck of the iceboat, hands bound behind him, he pondered her reaction. "Do you want a divorce?"

"You really are an idiot," she snapped. "Or maybe just a man. I know that you love me, really and for certain. I'd rather be married to an idiot who I know truly loves me than a genius who thinks of me as little more than an ornament to his own brilliance. Or," she added, "just because I'm beautiful and rich."

"I'm rich, too," he protested.

"Lot of good it does us now." She ruminated. "Both of our families have the means to ransom us. That won't matter because it's likely we'll freeze to death before the necessary arrangements can be made." It was not necessary for her to see the color-coded heat-sensitive readout that was part of the fabric of her daysuit's left arm to know that the integrated chemical reaction that kept the suit warm would have run the last of its reactive course by morning. Then they would find themselves clad in suits that kept out the wind but not the bitter cold. If the temperature hovered a few degrees below freezing they might still be able to survive.

This, however, was Tran-ky-ky—not some comfortable ski resort on one of the developed worlds. Native clothing—a lot of native clothing—would certainly help. How distant lay the abode of the Virin? Could they get there before they froze?

By evening they were far from the little island of the hot springs—and presumably also well beyond the area likely to be checked by any wandering search parties. Within the failing suits a cold-induced lethargy had begun to take hold. In this reduced state of awareness they were barely able to appreciate the stunning sunset as Tran-ky-ky's star, warm and bright as Earth's but more distant, began to set in a sky as stridently blue as cornflower sapphire. The glare of sunlight ricocheting off the surface of the ice ocean forced them to look away.

Leastwise it did until one of their captors left his position aft and walked forward to the starboard railing. Halting there he squinted into the distance, toward the setting sun, before letting out a roar that made even the two humans jump. In response, his comrades flew into a frenzy of action. Racing back to the stern, Draz-hode joined the steersman in leaning hard on the tiller. The iceboat heeled over dangerously, its starboard runner actually rising up off the ice. Running to that side, two of the crew grabbed pika-pina ropes and heeled out, lending their weight to the ascending side of the craft. Slowly, gradually, the runner in the air dropped down until it once more was in contact with the ice.

The rest of the crew was racing to break out a second triangular sail. It was not quite a spinnaker, but it did allow the iceboat to put on additional speed. The sturdy craft was traveling with the wind nearly full behind it now. Draz-hode's intent was clearly to make speed as opposed to maintaining his original course. The reason for this soon became apparent.

They were being chased by a mountain—and a forested one at that.

Arik could see Jen's eyes widen behind her face shield. He wondered if she could see his. Were they as reflective of the shock he was feeling at the sight of what was bearing down on them? The alarm evident in the actions and expressions of their captors was hardly a consolation. If those sailing the iceboat died, so would their involuntary passengers.

One of the reasons he and Jen had come to Tran-ky-ky was to observe the local wildlife—but not like this.

Closing on the fleeing iceboat was an enormous lump of ivory-hued flesh. Slashes of gray and pale blue streaked its deeply ribbed flanks. What at a distance had appeared to be trees turned out to be wind-blown growths of another kind. Evolution had caused a dozen or so huge fins to grow wider, higher, and thinner. No longer required by nature to push water, they now caught air like so many macrobiotic blades. The monster had no limbs. It had no eyes or ears. What it did have was a dozen or more integral "sails" protruding from its back and sides. Also a cavernous mouth large and dark enough to swallow the fleeing iceboat whole.

Projecting forward and out from the top of the blunt-headed alien atrocity was a distinctive fleshy organ the size of a bus and the color of an irritated blister. Eyeing the bizarre growth, Arik found himself wondering how the creature could locate prey without eyes to see, ears to hear, or nostrils to smell. What senses were left?

This was Tran-ky-ky, he reminded himself. Where everything was frozen solid except for isolated areas of volcanism and—living, organic beings. Not being versed in the tenets of exobiology he could not be certain, but it seemed to him a reasonable assumption the massive protuberance that dominated the head of the oncoming creature might have evolved to detect the heat given off by living things.

Ironically, while the energetic kurgal of Virin were radiating heat like mad, the predator might not be able to sense either him or Jen because their body heat was bottled within their daysuits. Under different circumstances, it might utterly ignore them.

Despite the best efforts of Draz-hode and his crew the gap continued to close between the fleeing iceboat and that enormous mouth. It seemed impossible that something so massive, florid, and alien could travel so fast. What on earth—or rather on ice—enabled it to do so? It was not until it was almost upon them that the fading daylight allowed him to make out the layer of glistening liquid that bubbled and frothed around the creature's underside.

He remembered what little he and Jen had been able to learn about Tran-ky-ky's remarkable fauna. The key to survival of many species was the presence in their blood of highly evolved complex glycoproteins. These naturally occurring organic antifreezes kept the bodily fluids of everything from the lowliest ice-burrower to the Tran themselves from freezing when temperatures dropped precipitously. He could now see for himself that when exuded from special organs located in the monster's underside, they could also be employed for purposes of lubrication. The monster produced and secreted a glycoproteinetic fluid that provided a continuously replenished low-friction liquid cushion between itself and the ice. Or at least it did so when it needed to make speed to capture food.

Some predators relied on venom to snare their prey, others on natural glues, others on extensible tongues or claws. This was the first he had seen that relied on slime.

Realizing that despite their best efforts they were about to be overtaken, two of the crew disappeared into the central cabin. They re-emerged moments later bearing armfuls of spears. Arik could not imagine the metal-tipped shafts having much effect against the looming monster. He wished only that his and Jen's hands were not bound. Not that it really mattered. Even if the creature did not eat them, even if it smashed the iceboat but subsequently ignored them, they would be marooned out on the vastness of the open ice ocean, unable to walk to a destination even if one happened to be in sight.

Then, abruptly and unexpectedly, the gargantuan predator veered off to the right. Spears in hand, the two Tran looked on in bewildered silence as the predator pulled up alongside them. It made no move to swallow, crush, or otherwise attack the iceboat. Holding onto the tiller for dear life, Draz-hode and his steersman maintained their present course. They did not want to do anything to startle or disturb the speeding hulk that had inexplicably drawn harmlessly alongside. In any case, changing direction would have meant losing wind and therefore sacrificing speed.

The monster began to drift away to port. On board the iceboat the baffled but relieved Tran allowed themselves to relax ever so slightly. It was then that the giant landed in their midst.

Gray beard flying in the wind, face shield flipped up in defiance of the elements, he had leaped from behind one of the monster's stiff-spined sails with a pistol clasped in his massive left hand. Shod in boots and not fur, his enormous feet were devoid of ice-cutting chiv. Spears flew and swords were drawn. The iceboat was crewed by six warriors of the Virin, bold and true. In such close quarters the single modern weapon brandished by the arriving apparition did not enjoy the advantage it would have held at a distance.

On the other hand, Arik saw as he did his best to stay out of the way, the new arrival was taller even than the Tran, and far more stout. The man stood well over two meters tall and must have weighed close to two hundred kilos. This explained how he was able to pick up one warrior and throw him into a pair of his companions as easily as Arik would have tossed a ball.

One of the walloped was the steersman, who had remained at his post. Struck senseless, he fell forward onto the tiller. The iceboat promptly heeled hard over to starboard. With the remaining Virin occupied in trying to swarm the giant there was no one to haul out on the lines. The iceboat's starboard runner came up, up off the ice. Arik felt himself losing his balance, falling, and rolling helplessly down the now sharply tilting deck. Somewhere nearby, Jen screamed.

Darkness arrived before the sun had time to set.

A LIGHT that was bright teased his consciousness back to wakefulness. Faintly, Arik remembered that a bright light was what dead people supposedly saw before they passed into nothingness or onward to another plane of existence. As his vision cleared he saw that the light was coming from a fire. That was probably *not* what dying people saw, he decided. Optimism restored, he sat up.

He was sitting on a piece of flat woody material. An unmoving Jen lay on another alongside him. As he cried out, a voice that was ridiculously deep but not ponderous addressed him from the other side of the crackling blaze.

"Take it easy, young feller-me-lad. She ain't dead. Dreaming maybe, but not dead."

Placing his hands on his spouse, Arik was able to reassure himself that the words spoke the truth. He was further persuaded when she began to moan softly. At that point he thought it might be expeditious to have a closer look at the source of the voice.

Seated on the far side of the fire the giant who had leaped from the back of the monster onto the deck of the iceboat fed another piece of that shattered craft into the blaze. Moonglow highlighted the rest of the nearby wreckage. The spectral pile of splintered pika-pedan glittered with ice crystals. Of the monster that had chased them down there was no sign.

"September," the big man rumbled around a mouthful of food.

"Actually," Arik replied as he tried to get comfortable on the rough board that elevated his backside above the treacherous ice, "I think it's still July."

The giant let out a snort. "No, feller-me-lad—I'm September. You can call me Skua. Don't know why I should let you, though. By rights you at least owe me proper formalities."

"We owe you everything, I should think, Mr. Sep—Skua. You saved our lives."

"I've gone and saved your behinds, anyway." The big man grunted through his flaring gray beard. Barely detectible beneath overhanging brows, his eyes were as blue as the sky of Tran-ky-ky. "As to your lives, those remain hanging in the balance unless we can get you back to Brass Monkey before you freeze. Tomorrow we'll know if it's all one way or all the other."

Jen blinked and sat up sharply. Arik was delighted to see that the integrity of her daysuit had not been compromised and that she appeared to be unhurt. As for himself, he was bruised from head to toe, but nothing seemed to be broken. Hugging Jen tightly to him as she put both hands to her head, he looked back at the giant.

"You sound upset."

"Upset?" Arik thought the big man's gaze was going to cut right through him. "'Pon my word, young feller-me-lad, you've no notion of what you've cost me, do you?"

Arik swallowed. Had they been saved from the Virin of kurgal only to find themselves in the hands of a madman of their own species? "Whatever it is, sir, my wife and I will do our best to make it up to you if you'll just help us to get back to the outpost."

"Bollocks and botheration!" the giant snapped. "What I should have done was left the both of you fools to ice cube yourselves out here. You've cost me time, is what you've cost me. How d'you expect to pay that back?" He turned suddenly wistful. "I was all set to take transport away on the same ship that brought you here. Now I expect it has vacated orbit and gone on its merry changeover way."

"No it hasn't." Returned to full awareness once more, Jen spoke up.

The giant glanced over at her. "No offense, young lass, but I don't see any KK-drive vessel out this way flouting its schedule on my behalf."

"Not your behalf, sir. On ours." She favored Arik with an unexpectedly affectionate look. "My new idiot husband and I are not particularly important people, but we do come from families of some importance. I don't think the ship will leave without us, or at least not until our deaths should be confirmed."

Skua September glared at her. "I'm afraid you have a disproportionately elevated opinion of yourself, young miss. It has been my humble experience that starships don't hang around waiting on tardy passengers. No matter who their daddy is."

Daring to raise her face shield, she flashed blue eyes of her own at him. "I don't like to think that wealth makes me arrogant. Just realistic."

Arik stepped hurriedly back into the conversation. "We might anyway have a few days before the ship's captain feels he has to depart. How soon can you get us back to the station?"

September considered. "I'll do my best, young-feller-me-lad. Out of personal interest as much for your sake. I didn't come out here with the intention of returning with a block of honeymooning ice in tow." He smiled. "Yes, I know about that. I just wouldn't hold out hope that you'll be leaving this paradise quite as soon as you'd like."

"Whatever happens, we're in your debt, Skua."

"Your goddamn debt's got nothing to do with it. The sooner we get back, the better the chance I have of making that ship."

"If you don't mind my asking," Arik began as he started to shiver uncontrollably, "how did you find us? And that creature you were riding …?"

Rising, the giant disappeared into the darkness. When he returned he was carrying an armful of rough-hewn Tran clothing. "Here, put these on as best you can over those failing daysuits. You'll find the native attire surprisingly insulating." Sitting back down beside the fire, he used a Tran knife to slice off another chunk of charred meat and shove it into his mouth. Melting grease dribbled off his lips to stain his beard.

"When you didn't check back in to your accommodations last night or return your rented iceboat, Ms. Stanhope—she's the resident Commonwealth commissioner for Tran-ky-ky—sent out a couple of skimmers to look for you. By law and Church edict that kind of technology is not supposed to travel beyond Brass Monkey until this world's application for associate membership has been vetted and approved. Given the circumstances, she decided to allow an exception so a proper search could be conducted. Since she has less than half a dozen operatives assigned to her staff, the commissioner also asked for Tran and human volunteers to join the search.

"Unsurprisingly, the local Tran have no interest in wasting time looking for a couple of humans dim-witted enough to lose themselves out on the ice. Those more noble Tran who might have taken the time aren't around right now. They're back home north of here in Arsudun. Needless to say, no humans volunteered—they're not dumber than the natives. However, you don't get to be a Resident Commissioner, even for an ends-of-the-galaxy iceball like Tran-ky-ky, unless you know how to manipulate hearts and minds. A few of my friends and I have invested quite a bit of time and energy in helping the locals reach the point where they qualify to apply for associate membership in the Commonwealth. Commissioner Stanhope, the old dear, bluntly pointed out that the deaths of an attractive young couple such as yourselves following so soon upon such a submission would reflect badly on the formal application." He spat to one side. "Politics!"

"So she appealed to your sense of honor," Jen remarked.

"'Pon my word she did. Fortunately for you, that was not all she relied upon. Other words were spoken. 'Reward' being among them, I decided it was worth burning a day or two looking for you.

"Having spent some time on this world and acquired an understanding of certain of its ways, I managed to track your wandering iceboat's tracks to a hot spring island. There I found evidence pointing to the recent visit of a clandestine native hunting party. Also human spoor, but no sign of your rented craft or you. Knowing what I do about the Tran, I came to some assumptions. Iceboat tracks leading straightaway from Arsudun and not just from the island confirmed my suspicions.

"That presented a new problem. I knew that no matter how fast and low I came up in a modern skimmer on you and your new friends, they would have ample time to put knives to your throats before I could be certain of taking all of them out, or even talking to them. I was at a bit of a loss how to proceed until I came across the solitary tarqan.

"Now, a tarqan's dangerous when it's on the move, but not so much when it's feeding. I managed to sneak up on that one. Adept Tran can pretty well steer them where they want them to go by applying heat to certain areas of their body. I had some chemical instant heat paks in the skimmer's supply locker. They did the job. I knew the hunting party that had taken you would respond defensively to an approach by a tarqan, but they wouldn't connect its presence to you or to a rescue attempt. In the fading daylight I was able to draw close without being seen. After that I was able to get in among them before they had time to realize what was happening.

"I would've preferred to stay on the tarqan and pick them off from a distance, but I knew that before I could get them all," he concluded as casually as if describing a day's excursion in a park, "they would have had plenty of time to cut off your heads."

He bit back down into whatever it was that he had cooked over the fire. Arik's stomach chose that moment to say hello and, by the way, he was starving, and could he perhaps do something about it? Jen was undoubtedly no better off.

"Could I ask you ..." He indicated the hunk of well-seared flesh. It smelled wonderful. "Jen and I haven't had anything to eat since yesterday." He tried hard not to salivate, knowing that if he did so dripping saliva would freeze hard to his lower lip and chin.

"Bless my soul, I've forgotten my manners." From the lump he was chewing on, September promptly carved off slices of cooked flesh for both of them.

Arik bit hungrily into his. Next to him Jen was chowing down with an enthusiasm that was anything but ladylike. With a flavor that was somewhere between pork and undercooked beef, the blackened flesh was delicious.

"I'm surprised that you would have room in your backpack for raw meat." Arik discovered he was downright ravenous. "Though on second thought I suppose keeping it frozen isn't a problem here."

"It ain't frozen, feller-me-lad," September informed him casually. "It's fresh."

"Fresh?" Jen stared at the giant, her slab of seared flesh halfway to her lips. "Fresh what? Some local food?"

"In a manner of speaking, young lass." September nodded in the direction of the destroyed Virin iceboat. "In a difficult situation on a world like this one makes use of whatever is available. Not just here on

Tran-ky-ky. I've been in awkward circumstances before and if there's one thing I've learned in the course of a tolerably long lifetime, it's that meat is meat."

Rising slightly from his sitting position, Arik was able to get a better look at what lay just beyond the fire. Along with the giant's pack and pistol he was able to make out a larger, more irregular object. It was the corpse of the Virin commander Draz-hode.

It had been neatly and very professionally butchered.

Slowly, he removed a half-chewed piece of meat from his mouth. In the flickering light from the fire it looked exactly like any other piece of cooked meat. Next to him, Jen had not so much as paused in her voracious masticating despite September's matter-of-fact identification of what it was that she was consuming.

This is not impossible, he admonished himself sternly. All you had to do was turn off your brain while leaving your digestive system running. Slipping the meat back between his lips he resumed chewing while simultaneously doing his best to stop thinking. His stomach thanked him.

To help take his mind off the fact that he was violating two and possible four of the principle canons of contemporary civilized behavior, he confronted the giant with a question that had been bothering him for a while now.

"Why are we sitting here eating in the dark and the cold like this? Why haven't you signaled your skimmer to come fetch us and take us back to the station?"

By way of reply September unfastened one of his sturdy survival suit's external pockets. Removing a small handful of electronics, he tossed them across the fire. Arik had to drop his deviant steak to make the catch. Still, several of the pieces missed his fingers to scatter on the ice. Too many pieces, he thought with sudden unease.

"This component is broken," he murmured as he and Jen studied the debris.

September nodded. "Sure can't fool you, young feller-me-lad. During the dust-up, that module took the full force of a blow from a Tran battleaxe. The flat side of the axe, fortunately. Only bruised me, but it sure made a mess of my communicator."

Jen gaped at him. "So we're marooned again? Except that now there's three of us, and we're that much further from Brass Monkey?"

"It is a bit of a hike back, yes." Setting his food aside, September reached behind him and hauled his backpack into the firelight. From its depths he withdrew a pair of enormous ice skates. The blades were not stone, and had been fashioned out of duralloy or some similar metal.

"Local government issue. Wish I'd had them with me a year ago." Illustrating how they fit, he slipped one over the integrated right boot of his survival suit. Wiggling it caused the triple blades to catch the light of the fire. It dawned on Arik that the skate's design had been modeled after a Tran foot.

"Special coating baked onto the blades reduces friction to next to nothing," September told them proudly. "You can make pretty good time with a pair of these. And with this." Digging into the pack once more he pulled out a thin sheet of carboflex. A contiguous seal was visible along the edge.

"This attaches to a survival suit. Fits in a roll over your arms and across your back. Mimics Tran dan." Extending both long arms out to his sides he made slightly awkward flapping motions. "Catches the wind and propels you across the ice. Just like one of the natives."

"Clever." Jen eyed the commodious pack. "Where's ours?"

"Well now, lass, that does present a bit of a problem. This is emergency gear. It's intended to allow someone who knows what they're doing to maybe make it back to civilization in the event of a complete skimmer or iceboat breakdown. I'm afraid I only have the one set, for me."

The newlyweds exchanged a glance. "Then what are we to do?" Arik asked. "Wait here for you to return with your skimmer?"

"Hardly. There are enough fancy ice sculptures in Brass Monkey without adding the two of you to the gallery. You're coming with me."

"How?" Jen contemplated their rescuer's considerable size. "Can you carry us?"

"Not while trying to stay upright on the ice while maneuvering artificial dan. But in the course of the past year I've gotten pretty good at improvising."

The flat ice skid the big man threw together from the wreckage of the Virin iceboat was uncomfortable and fragile. At any moment Arik expected it to come apart under him and Jen. Salvaged pika-pedan ropes attached it to September's waist. With his arms held outspread and the artificial dan attached at wrist, arms, sides and waist, he could both pull the sled and catch the ubiquitous wind.

Though they started out slow, soon the three of them were all but flying across the ice. Buried beneath appropriated Tran clothing and eyeing September through his protective face mask, Arik wondered how long the giant could keep his arms extended straight out to the sides. Long enough, it developed, for the skid's two recumbent passengers to feel more bumps and jolts than they had before in their entire lives up to that point.

By the time they reached the small cold spire of an island where September had parked his skimmer, the both of them were sore from head to heel. Though their rented daysuits had by now chemically redlined, the layers of Tran fur and leather taken from their dead abductors had kept them from freezing. Aching and exhausted, they stumbled gratefully into the waiting warmth of the skimmer's interior. With the inadequate pilot's seat groaning beneath his weight, September set a course back to the Commonwealth outpost.

There they discovered that the giant had been right about something else. Commercial KK-drive ships did not linger on behalf of passengers who missed their assigned shuttle. Not even on behalf of rich ones. The next starship was not due to visit Tran-ky-ky for a month. Until then the newlyweds would have to listen like everyone else to their rescuer grumble and complain as he stalked the heated halls of the station. They would have to endure this just as they would have to endure surroundings that were considerably less appealing than those they had planned to enjoy on the balance of their travels. At least, however, they were alive and had each other.

Even if it was for as frigid a honeymoon as any two citizens of the Commonwealth had ever experienced.

5

Consigned

I've spent a fair amount of time underwater. It's beautiful down there. In fact, one might almost say that life is much better down where it's wetter, except that's copyrighted, so I won't say it.

When you emerge from the sea after a long time, say more than an hour, a great deal of heat has been sucked out of your body. You are also dehydrated. You're inordinately grateful for a drink, a dry towel, and a chance to stand in the tropical sun. It's a very small but genuine heavenly feeling.

On the other hand, depending on how you have evolved, the reverse might be true....

"WHY ARE you so determined to go to Hell?"

Crouched down behind the fold of reef, Menno kept his bubbles small and deliberately unobtrusive as he whispered a reply to Codan. "All my life I was told that I was destined to go to Hell. It was a determination that I accepted willingly. What has always astonished me is that no one else shares my desire to do so."

Holding his spear steady as he floated parallel to the sandy bottom, his friend spoke while intently eyeing the parade of passing polosto. "How awkward it must be for you to find that the rest of the world is so terribly afflicted with sanity."

"Always the sarcastic one." Menno joined his friend in patiently watching and waiting as the school of unaware potential prey continued to drift nearer. "Sarcastic and apathetic."

"I am not at all apathetic," Codan assured the other hunter. "I am adamantly opposed to the very notion. Didn't you ever realize that the suggestion was not to be taken literally? People are often told to go to Hell. None of them ever takes it as a personal challenge. At least, none until you, my friend." Upon concluding this observation he exploded forward over the top of the reef and thrust madly with his spear. With their cover thus broken, Menno had little choice but to follow.

He had to admit that Codan had chosen the moment well. The polosto had come in very close to the reef, enabling both hunters to spear good-sized individuals before the school could flee. As the impaled quarry writhed on the polished lengths of zek shell, unable to flee or reach around far enough to bite the hunters, the two Tyry began eating their prey alive. There was, after all, nothing a true Tyry enjoyed more than eating. Beginning with the tentacles, a true delicacy, the pair soon worked their way down to the half-consumed polostos' internal superstructure which consisted of a single expanding spiral of bone.

The rest of the carcasses and all of the polostos' internal organs were saved and stowed in drag-sacks of woven absab weed. These would be towed home to be distributed among the members of both males' extended families. Once the two hunters had eaten their fill they turned away from the outer reef to begin the long swim homeward. Coordinating their departure from the reef with the changing of the current allowed them to make steady and relatively easy progress.

"Why don't you come with me?" Using a right-side tentacle to flick aside a persistent cluster of parasitic keleth worms, Menno drifted a little closer to his friend. His strong, broad, four-lobed tail made short work of those keleth who persisted.

"What, to Hell?" Using one webbed tentacle, Codan gestured disparagingly. "I wish you would drop this enduring mania, Menno. It was already becoming tiresome years ago." Using his spear, he prodded a likely-looking hole as he swam past the opening. If it had been home to a tasty foudan, the angry invertebrate within would have displayed itself and its anger immediately, an appearance that would have led to its becoming an instant appetizer. "Much as certain members of the community might wish it, you are not going to Hell, however much you persist in pretending to continue to humor their requests."

"Well, don't say I didn't give you the chance." With a half flip of his tail, Menno accelerated out ahead of his friend.

Turning his head slightly to the right so that he could focus one eye completely on the other Tyry, Codan flicked his own tail and caught up. "What are you talking about? What 'chance'?"

Menno slowed deliberately, dropping down beneath his friend in a gesture of polite deference. They were very close now to the place he had chosen for the attempt. "I'm going. This evening." Raising two of his four webbed tentacles, he extended them rightward. "There."

Backfinning, Codan halted in mid-water. "Now you're scaring me, Menno. A joke's a joke, but you're not bubbling laughter." Having turned, he now found himself staring in the direction his friend had indicated.

Instead of being composed of sand or reef or storm debris, the indicated area was smooth and solid; all rock, with nothing growing or hiding on it. Other than a distinct greenish tinge, its most notable characteristic was a remarkably unbroken upward sloping.

"I have been all the way to the end," Menno declared proudly. "To the terminus. To the place where the real world ends. The slope continues on and on, the greenstone ascending steadily until it breaks the sky—and passes beyond it to enter Hell. I am convinced of this."

Turning away from the stony incline Codan gaped at his lifelong friend and hunting partner, turning to regard him first out of his left eye, then the right. "You're not joking, are you?"

"I am quite serious." Menno gazed back at him.

Coming close, Codan studied his companion's upper body. "Your eyes are clear and unfogged, so you have not been eating the purple kalis that grows in the lower caves. Your words are precise. Only your thoughts, it seems, betray any madness." Having rendered this opinion, Codan resumed swimming toward home.

Menno caught up to him easily. "Since others told me that I was destined to go there, I have always dreamed of being the first Tyry to visit Hell and return."

"Easy to visit." Codan gestured with his left tentacles. "Impossible to return."

"Not any longer. I have devised an apparatus."

That brought Codan up short in mid-water. "An apparatus?" He held up his spear. "*This* is an apparatus, and a very effective one. But it cannot get me to Hell and back. No artificial construct can do that."

"I have prepared for this all my life." Menno's tone was confident, assured. "You'll see. I will show you tomorrow morning. If you won't join me, will you at least come to observe? Without a credible witness there will be none to believe me."

"Bereave you, you mean." Reaching out, Codan draped a tentacle around his friend's upper body. "Be a sensible fellow. We've made a good catch, we're bringing back plenteous food to share around, and tomorrow is another bright and beautiful day. Enough of this talk of going to Hell." He made a gesture that was reflective of his innate sardonicism. "We all get there sooner or later anyway."

"If you won't come …" Menno's voice trailed off tersely as he thrust hard with his tail lobes.

"I didn't say that." Codan rushed to catch up. "I suppose I must attend. As a friend and hunter-brother. Someone has to be there to revive you."

"Thanks." Menno entwined one of his own tentacles around that of his friend. "As a moment of historical importance it will be in need of recording."

"A moment of hysterical importance," Codan corrected him—but gently, for he was truly and honestly concerned.

The morning of the following day dawned clear and sunny. The atmosphere was bright, cool, and devoid of current. A perfect day for visiting Hell, Menno assured his friend. Or rather, friends, for Codan had insisted on bringing Kedef along. In addition to being senior to both of the hunters, among the Tyry Kedef had an impeccable reputation for honesty. Whatever he reported would be believed. This was the reason Codan proffered for inviting him, anyway. In reality it was a subterfuge, a way for him to enlist the aid of a respected elder in trying to talk Menno out of what was seeming to be more and more an inescapable episode of insanity.

"Even if you could somehow enter Hell and survive there," Kedef was muttering as the three males swam parallel to one another in the direction of the greenstone slope, "you are sure to be eaten by a demon." He turned reflective. "I commend to you the tale of Ses-Haban."

Ses-Haban was a mythical Tyry of ancient times who had dared to swim high enough to gesture contemptuously at the inhabitants of Hell. According to the legend, he had thrust two tentacles completely out of the real world and into that terrible nether realm. What he sensed there was unknown, because as soon as he had done the unbelievable deed, a demon had promptly bitten off both intruding limbs.

Singled-minded of purpose and determined to fulfill the urge that had driven him since childhood, Menno would not be dissuaded. "Ses-Haban, if he existed, was unlucky."

"Ses-Haban, if he existed," Codan suggested brusquely, "was stupid."

"Where is this apparatus of which you have spoken?" the elder inquired. Codan did not try to conceal his surprise. Was Kedef showing interest?

"You will see it soon," Menno assured him. "I've had to work on it in secret, when away from the community." Having reached the flow of greenstone, he led them downslope. "Jeers and jibes do not bother me, but there are those whose fears exceed their common sense. Had they known what I was about they might have tried to interfere with my work." He twisted his upper body to look back the way they had come. "They might have tried to stop me."

"You can hardly blame people for fearing Hell," Codan reminded him.

"People fear that which they do not understand," the other hunter riposted.

"Often with good reason," Codan added. But this time, his friend did not respond.

The entrance to the small cave had been camouflaged with loose reef growth and rock. Working with all four of his tentacles, Menno dragged the rubble aside. From the dark interior he extracted a thick, perfectly transparent tuzaca shell. But it was not the classic spiral tuzaca shape. A deformity had produced a shell that took the form of an elongated bubble.

Kedef's tone as he studied the product of the younger Tyry's labors was admiring. Codan realized to his horror that the elder's presence was starting to have the opposite effect from what he had intended by inviting the older Tyry along in the first place.

"You have modified this." Kedef spoke with assurance as he eyed the unusually developed shell. "In several places, it would appear."

Gratification suffused Menno's reply. "Yes. See here, where I have smoothed the base after removing the animal?"

Kedef's tentacle ends tiptoed appraisingly over the exterior of the crystal-clear shell, stopping at a round opening. "And what is this hole for? It is not natural."

"No. I made it. That is where the voyoupa intestine goes."

Shells and intestines. Codan was beginning to wonder if he was going to have to use force to put a stop to this lunacy.

As he and Kedef looked on, Menno extracted another shell from the cavity in the rocks. This one had a lid. When opened, both sight and smell identified the shell's contents. Codan's tentacles recoiled. The shell contained chisith innards. Sticky and stinking, they were violently expelled by a chisith whenever it was attacked or disturbed. Enrobed in the ejected viscous strands, a preoccupied predator would pay no further attention to the chisith, allowing that simple creature to scoot safely on its way. What possible use could Menno have for such a pot of scavenged goo?

He proceeded to show them.

Working with a silicate spatula, he daubed chisith innards all over the upper part of his body, careful to stay above his tentacles but below his head. Taking up the large tuzaca, he then carefully pulled it down over his head so that its base rested against the painted line of chisith guts that now encircled his upper body. The gummy chisith gripped the base of the shell. Menno then brought out a long coil of voyoupa intestine. Additional chisith innards were pasted both inside and outside the round opening he had made in the tuzaca shell. One end of the intestine was passed through the hole. More chisith was added to the outside. Within seconds it had been tightly sealed in place.

"You perceive how this apparatus works?" he declared boldly. Though muted by the intervening shell that now enclosed his head and upper body, his words remained intelligible.

Codan had composed a choice response, but Kedef spoke first. "I think so, somewhat, but still ..." The elder's voice trailed off into uncertainty. "I am not sure I understand the proper function of the length of intestine."

"The principle is very simple." Clutching the coil of intestine in two tentacles, Menno used another to hold up the end. "There is no atmosphere in Hell. Only searing heat. Studies suggest that a Tyry can endure the increased temperature for some time before it begins to adversely affect the body. But this point is moot in the absence of breathable atmosphere." With his remaining free tentacle he reached up to tap the outside of the transparent tuzaca shell.

"The adhesive chisith insides form an atmospherically tight seal between my upper body and the tuzaca shell. The latter is presently full of perfectly breathable atmosphere. When I venture into airless Hell, I will carry my breathable atmosphere with me."

"It won't last you more than couple of minutes," Codan pointed out relentlessly. "Studies suggest *that*, too."

"Which difficulty brings us to the purpose of the voyouda intestine." Once again, Menno waved the open end. "There is a very small hole near the base of the tuzaca shell. Once in Hell, it will leak atmosphere. It is designed to do so. As exhausted atmosphere bleeds out, I will use the tube formed by this intestine to suck fresh atmosphere into the shell. Bad atmosphere out, good atmosphere in." He eyed the two other Tyry; one old and thoughtful, the other young and alarmed.

"What if this crazy setup fails on you?" Cedan demanded to know. "What if the chisith seal fails, letting the atmosphere inside the shell all out at once? What if you can't suck in fresh atmosphere fast enough to replace the old?"

"Then I will still have time enough to return to the real world." Menno's confidence had not deserted him. Indeed, Cedan thought, the closer his friend came to suicide the more assured he appeared to become. "I will only need a minute or two. If it comes to it, I can hold my breath longer than that."

"It is an astounding and bold notion." Kedef hovered in the water above the smooth greenstone, his tail moving lazily back and forth to hold him in position against the current.

Cedan turned on the elder. "You are not actually going to give your blessing to this madness?"

Turning to his left, Kedef eyed the younger Tyry with his left eye.

"It is not a matter of giving blessing or the withholding of it. Menno is of age. I cannot and would not try to stop him. Besides, everyone in the community knows he has spoken of a desire to fulfill the requests of many ever since his tail lobes were first formed." He looked back at the obviously proud Menno. "Triumph rewards the audacious."

"There is audacity," Cedan pointed out, "and then there is folly." But by this time Kedef was paying him no more attention than was his friend.

So thoroughly had things turned that Kedef helped Menno to secure the length of intestine to the hole in the tuzaca shell. Cedan refused to lend a tentacle to the final preparations. Even at the speed he could swim, it was too far to race back to the community to raise the alarm. He could only hope that the foredoomed experiment would not also destroy his friend.

When the last of the preparations were concluded, Menno turned a slow circle in the water. "How does it look?"

"Everything appears tight and secure, young boldness." Kedef's tone was full of admiration. "How is your breathing?"

Holding up the open end of the voyouda intestine, Menno waggled it back and forth. "No problem."

"Of course there's no problem," Cedan growled. "He's still in the real world." But it was not long until that boundary was being tested.

He and Kedef followed as far as they dared. They trailed behind the self-assured Menno as the latter swam upslope with even, powerful strokes of his tail. Soon they were in the shallows, and still Menno continued swimming. Onward and upward. Cedan realized that further pleading was of no use. His friend was determined to go through with this. It was, after all, the fulfillment of a life-long compulsion.

Drifting together side by side, he and Kedef watched in fascination as Menno kept swimming, swimming, just kept swimming, until all they could see was the hunter's lower body, then just his tail, and finally not even that. He was well and truly gone. Gone into Hell itself. But the end of the long coil of voyouda intestine trailed behind, whipping slowly back and forth in the slight current that marked the boundary between Hell and the real world.

"Do you think he's still alive?" Cedan finally asked after an interminable several moments had passed.

"I think he must be." There was wonderment in Kedef's voice. "If he had been eaten by a demon, then I would think the piece of voyouda would have fallen back into the water by now. A demon would either pull it out or let it go, but not maintain a constant length. Think of it! A Tyry, moving about in Hell itself, observing and recording for the first time! What tales your friend will have to tell us when he returns. What unprecedented sights he will have seen!"

Cedan said nothing.

More time passed. It seemed impossible that Menno could have survived so long beyond the sky. The waiting was taking its toll on both him and Kedef. They had been half rocked to sleep by the current when his eyes suddenly dilated sharply.

"There! By the Line of Otos, he's coming back!"

Upslope in front of them it was indeed the familiar shape of Menno that was coming in their direction. But something was wrong. The atmosphere-retaining tuzaca shell was still in place, glued securely to the hunter's upper body by the tough chisith innards. The upper end of the voyouda intestine was still sealed to the hole Menno had artfully drilled in the shell. Despite this, the intrepid explorer was not swimming normally. His tail was not moving. His tentacles as limp as strands of ncasa weed, he drifted partway toward them before being caught by the current.

Cedan and Kedef did not hesitate. Taking deep breaths in case something hellborn should come after them, they swam rapidly upward, grabbed hold of the motionless hunter, and dragged him down into deeper, safer water.

"Menno!" Cedan was tugging and flailing at the tuzaca shell. When it would not come loose, he pulled his knife from his waistwrap and used it to cut through the spongy, solidified chisith. With Kedef pulling, they soon had the shell off. Still Menno did not respond.

When he saw why, Cedan whirled and lost the undigested remnants of his morning meal.

Even the venerable Kedef was forced to momentarily turn away. Only when both had managed to overcome the initial shock were they able to turn back to Cedan's friend.

Menno was dead. That was immediately apparent. It was the particularly Hellish means of his passing that had so shocked them. The driven explorer's entire upper body was burned dark, as if it had been shoved into one of the underwater volcanic vents that dotted the far boundaries of the community's territory. His eyes had been boiled away. Cedan tried to imagine his friend under that kind of assault, reeling from the unexpected fiery pain as he struggled to make his way back into the water. With his eyes gone he had probably lost his way, and had only stumbled back into the real world when it was too late. Stumbled, or fallen and slid downslope.

But the tuzaca shell, full of cooling, soothing atmosphere, had survived intact and was still sealed in place. What had gone wrong?

"I cannot imagine," Kedef murmured in response to Cedan's query. "I have not the kind of specialized knowledge necessary to posit an answer to that question." Drifting in the water, the somber elder considered the dead, burned body. "Yet his lower body, beneath the shell, shows signs of only slight wrinkling. It is almost as if in some way the tuzaca shell that was necessary to sustain life somehow contributed to his destruction. If this attempt is to be repeated, the matter will require considerable further study."

"Further …?" Cedan gaped at the elder. "You don't mean that you're going to suggest that another Tyry try this?"

Kedef responded with a gesture that was difficult to interpret. "You are yet young, Cedan. A thing once tried is destined to be tried again. Wiser Tyry than you or I will discuss what has happened here today and seek ways of overcoming it. There will always be those who feel they have no choice but to push at the limits of the possible. There will always be those who from an early age will be urged to go to Hell, to the point where they come to regard it as their destiny."

Cedan was quiet for a long moment. When he spoke again, it was with renewed admiration for his deceased companion. "Well, all is not lost today. In his passing Menno has provided me with the opportunity to fulfill a long-held desire of my own. To eat a close friend."

Kedef gestured understandingly. "A laudable, if not especially revolutionary aspiration. I will assist with the hauling."

Together they towed the body of the dead explorer back to the community. The story of his valiant effort, temporary success, and subsequent demise was the occasion of much discussion and debate. In the end, the effort was accounted a modest success. After all, there were leftovers….

6

Cold Fire

As a tiny part of its education program, The National Science Foundation has a policy of sending one speaker a year up to Barrow (now Utqiagvik) Alaska to give talks to the students at the local schools. Being the northernmost community on the North American continent, Barrow (have some sympathy for my spellchecker—I'm going to continue to say Barrow) doesn't receive a lot of casual travelers. For the speaker in 2006 it was decided to invite a science-fiction writer instead of yet another scientist. I was asked if I would be interested. As a lover of far-away places, I accepted immediately, with one proviso: I wanted to go in the dead of winter, to experience the conditions.

So it was that in mid-December of that year I found myself winging from Fairbanks to Barrow, in pitch darkness. I was in seat 1A, which I thought from the numeration would put me in first class. What I learned upon boarding was that seat 1A was in the first row of coach halfway back in the plane, the front half of that particular Boeing 737 configuration being given over entirely to cargo (Alaska Airlines was the only US airline to fly this unique combi: they have since been retired in favor of separate aircraft for cargo and passengers). This was important because there are no roads to Barrow, only twenty-six miles of town road, all of which dead-end in the tundra. So a lot of cargo arrives via air. I also learned that the temperature is higher inside the food freezers of the local markets than it is outside the local markets. And much, much more.

Some of which found its way into the following story, which I wrote after returning home....

.   .   .

BY FOUR PM the arctic sky was filled with a haunting wispy green that twisted and writhed in front of the stars like the fluttering wing feathers of a frightened tropical songbird, and Morgan knew he was freezing to death.

As if that wasn't bad enough, he was sure the wolf was laughing at him.

It stood above him, silhouetted by starlight on the rim of the depression where he had sought shelter and found only death. Little puffs of laughter emerged from the lips of the formidable gray eminence, crystalizing in the air before the wind carried them off to the north. They were only congregations of breath; soft, anxious, canid exhalations. But in the haze and daze that was progressively smothering his thoughts, Morgan was sure it was laughter. When the powerful predator was through chuckling at his predicament, it would begin to eat him. Gazing up from where the heavy steel leg trap pinned him to the bottom of what he had hoped would be a sheltering hollow in the tundra, he imagined that the eyes of the wolf were like emeralds lit from within.

Might as well be eaten, he thought resignedly, by something beautiful.

It was not supposed to be this way. He had set off from Barrow with his cameras and a big thermos of hot coffee and another of rich chicken soup in hopes of capturing some panoramic scenes of the deep arctic winter. It was mid-December on the North Slope, a time when only the most fitful illumination between ten in the morning and two in the afternoon glazed the landscape like glistening honey. Before and thereafter, the sky was as black as the oil that gushed out of the ground at Prudhoe Bay, far to the east. When some of the staff at the hotel in Barrow had expressed reservations about him traveling alone out into the shadowy tundra, he had smiled cheerfully and assured them he had plenty of fuel to make it to the little village of Atqasuk, only sixty miles distant. His all-weather GPS would keep him from getting lost, and he had plenty of experience on snowmobiles (or snow machines, as they called them up here) back in Wisconsin.

Except ... this wasn't Wisconsin, the satchel holding his GPS unit and cell phone had been crushed when he had dumped and damaged the snow machine halfway between Barrow and Atqasuk, and both the coffee and chicken soup had long since been consumed and had dissipated their life-sustaining heat throughout his bruised body hours ago. Then the wind had come up. He had sought temporary shelter in the fortuitous depression. Perhaps the wolf had come seeking shelter there as well, only to find that today the familiar protective hollow was offering board as well as room. A logical place, Morgan had realized too late, for a trapper to set his steel.

He was out of food, out of drink, out of hope. Very soon now, with the questing, relentless cold beginning to work its way through his multiple layers of clothing, he would be out of time. The irony was that the North Slope was experiencing a heat wave. The temperature when he had left town had been almost five degrees above zero Fahrenheit. He had seen Inupiaq women grocery shopping in socks and flip-flops.

It didn't matter. Even without the wind, he would still freeze to death. And it felt much colder now. A dry, still pain had begun to numb his muscles and seep into his bones. Coming in slower, longer heaves, his breath crackled like breakfast cereal.

Emerald eyes, burning as they came closer. Fixated and hungry. The two-legged prey in the depression showed no sign of trying to flee. Baring her teeth, the solitary female prepared to pass the word to her pack. Morgan felt himself losing consciousness as a chill, dark blanket began to settle over him.

Something sharper than a snap of thumb and finger re-ignited his hearing. A wheeze of snow puffed skyward just to the left of the wolf's front paw. Her head came up, the fire in her eyes flickered, and she turned and bolted. Had she ever been there? Or had he imagined her? As his thoughts spun and mixed with the swirling snow around him, Morgan could not help but lament the passing of what would have been a great picture. *If* he'd had one of his cameras with him. *If* he'd had the strength to aim it and take the shot. If he had been able to lift his head. He heard a voice.

"Damn. Missed her."

Thump, shuffle, thump. Retreating to the safety of childhood, Morgan remembered the muffled sound his favorite stuffed dinosaur had made every time he had punched the crap out of it. A terrible pressure left his leg as the jaws of the steel trap parted and his leg was gently but firmly raised and laid aside. Then he was in motion; rising and sitting up, though not of his own accord. Strong arms beneath his own, short and powerful like the concrete pillars that held buildings above the permafrost in Barrow, were lifting him up.

"Come on, man. Help me. I don't want to have to drag you all the way."

Rejuvenated by the sound of another human, and one exuding soft-voiced confidence as well, Morgan summoned reserves he had long since given up for lost, and in an instant of wonderment found himself again on two feet.

Half awake, half dead, unsure which way the balance was tilting, he leaned on the shorter man as they stumbled out of the hollow. Instead of a bright red snowsuit like the photographer wore, his unexpected savior was clad in a traditional heavy parka of dark blue. Colorful abstract embroidery decorated the sleeves and hem. The neck ruff was of wolf, perhaps a relative of the female who had been about to make a meal of the visitor from Wisconsin. The bottom hem, wrists, and hood were trimmed with wolverine fur, which strongly resists freezing even when wet. Rendered harmless by needlework, a set of threatening claws hung close to the zipper.

Ahead of them a shape loomed out of the wind and dark. Another snow machine, lean and mean but equipped with all the necessary gear for checking a winter trapline. At that moment it represented the most exquisite example of modern technology Morgan had ever set eyes upon. In his sudden anxiety to reach it, he stumbled against his rescuer. Neither fell. It was like falling against a soft, two-legged boulder.

"If you're going to die," the man shouted jovially above the wind, "at least wait until we get to the house. If I have to drag you behind the machine, it will make for one ugly corpse."

He helped the feeble Morgan onto the back of the vehicle. Even through the all-encompassing numbness that pervaded his body, the photographer could feel that the seat beneath him was uneven. Looking down, he saw that much of the space that was supposed to accommodate his butt was presently occupied by the bodies of several arctic hares and a white fox.

"Can you hang on?"

"What?"

Settling into the driver's seat, the hunter raised his voice. "Can you hang on? It's about ten miles to the house."

Unable to speak, the exhausted photographer nodded. It was sufficient. Adjusting his snow goggles, his stocky savior positioned himself. To Morgan, the Chicago Philharmonic doing Beethoven never made music as fine as the throaty roar of the snow machine's engine rumbling to life. A moment later men and machine were accelerating across the murky, ice-bound landscape.

"I'm Albert Tungarook!" the man yelled back at his passenger. "What happened to you?"

Gasping weakly, leaning forward, his eyes shut tight against the freezing wind as he pressed his face against the blue parka, Morgan explained. The driver nodded comprehendingly.

"Lucky for you I come along. From the looks of it, I figure you were about two minutes from becoming a wolfsicle. Sorry I didn't get her, though." He nodded at his passenger's seat. "Try to stay off the fox. It's frozen and can't bleed, but you don't want to ride halfway with a femur up your ass."

Ten miles. Ten miles of bumping, jouncing, bone-jarring anguish on the uneven tundra. Tungarook dodged ditches that were like zippers in the earth and sped over frozen ponds as easily as Morgan would have negotiated a sunlit highway back home. How the hunter found his way in the darkness and the flat frozen terrain Morgan did not know. The man never looked once at an instrument of any kind. There was no sun. There were no landmarks. But there were familiar constellations, and ribbons of waving, hypnotic aurora overhead to tie the stars together.

He was sure he was dead or dreaming, or dreaming of death, when he saw the pillar of green fire.

Green tinged with red actually. And purple, and a little blue. It plunged out of the black night like the lambent finger of an unseen genie. Hissing softly, it spilled with alacrity upon a small house set beside a frozen stream. Behind a single triple-paned window a more familiar yellow light beckoned, soft and familiar. All that was needed to complete the bucolic impossibility was wood smoke curling aesthetically upward from a brick chimney. But there was no chimney, brick or otherwise, and for hundreds of miles around no wood to fuel it had there been one.

He passed out against the back of Albert Tungarook, and dreamt of postcard nirvanas.

THE AROMA of something wonderful wrapped in steam brought him back to awareness. In a moment he was tasting as well as smelling it. Hot chocolate. It burned his lips. He didn't care. He would not have traded it for the amphoraed ambrosia of Zeus on Olympus.

Opening his eyes, he saw a round brown face gazing concernedly down at his own. When he met her gaze, the girl smiled. Where the eyes of the wolf had burned, hers sparkled. She inclined the blue rim of the heavy ceramic mug to his lips again, carefully. Reaching up, he took it from her and smiled back. To his surprise, his hands did not tremble.

Rising from the side of the couch where he lay entombed beneath several thick wool blankets, she turned and called out.

"Father, he's awake!" Clad in jeans and hoodie, the stocky sixteen-year old looked back down at him. "Excuse me. I've got to finish charging the batteries."

Father and daughter passed wordlessly in a doorway. *Batteries*, Morgan found himself thinking as he fought to sip and not chug the mug's delicious, steaming contents. Electric heat. That explained the almost oppressive warmth of the room in which he found himself.

But not the pillar of green fire. Nothing explained that, except perhaps delirium.

His own mug in hand, Tungarook settled himself down in a nearby overstuffed chair. It looked as old as it did comfortable. "Good. You're alive. Now you have a fine story to tell when you get home. Better even than pretty pictures. And I can tell my wife about the dumb white guy who let himself get caught out on the tundra when Casey and I go back to Barrow."

A sudden, unpleasant thought caused Morgan to swallow. "Frostbite?"

The hunter pursed his lips. "I don't think so. I checked you pretty close when we got you out of your clothes and under the blankets. There's a little blackening on a couple of toes, but I don't think you'll lose them." He smiled. "Of course, if you did have them amputated, that would give you proof for your story."

The photographer nodded and sat up. "I think I'd rather keep my toes and invite disbelief. Where are we?"

"In my living room."

For the first time since he had set out from Barrow on the ill-starred trip, Morgan found himself grinning. His mouth hurt. "You know what I mean."

"We're about halfway between Barrow and Atqasuk, but way north of the snow machine track everybody uses."

Morgan nodded slowly, sipping. "I broke my bike, my phone, everything. I was trying to hike back."

His host dropped his smile. "You never would have made it. Where I found you was way northwest of the track. Of course, when you hit the ocean you could have followed it to town. If you had better clothes and enough food and hot drink to keep you for a week or so. If you hadn't started out onto the ice. If."

The walls of the tightly sealed little house, Morgan noted, were decorated with framed pictures and other bric-a-brac. No animal heads or skins. Locals hunted for subsistence, not for sport. "I thought the wolf had me."

"Almost," Tungarook offered cheerfully. "You're just lucky a white bear didn't come across you." He nodded to his right. "They're probably all in Barrow, rummaging the dumpsters behind Pepe's or Arctic Pizza."

It was quiet in the room for a while. Wordlessly, Morgan held out his empty mug. Tungarook refilled it from the big white pitcher that sat on a coffee-table hand-made from a single piece of gnarled driftwood hauled from the nearby river. As the hunter sat back down, Morgan happened to glance out the window. A faint but distinct greenish glow stained the thin layer of snow outside. Eyes widening, he nearly shot off the couch. The sudden effort left him dizzy, but standing. He staggered to the window. There was no mistaking it: a flickering green light was turning the frozen crystals the color of lime sorbet.

Quickly at his side, Tungarook tried to ease his guest back onto the couch.

"Not so fast, man. You're still pretty weak. You'll hurt yourself."

The photographer succeeded in raising an arm to gesture outside. "Don't you see that?"

The hunter glanced out the window. "See what?"

Morgan looked down at his host. "I'm not delirious. Not now.

Something's casting a green glow on the snow." Turning and tilting his head back, he eyed at the low ceiling. "I saw something like it but much stronger when we were coming in. Stronger than a searchlight, it was. A bright, bright green, almost like the aurora."

Tungarook stared hard at his guest. Then the hunter exhaled a heavy sigh and stepped back, forcing Morgan to stand by himself. His fortitude strengthened by curiosity and chocolate, the photographer managed to remain upright.

"Not 'almost.'" His host made the correction reluctantly.

Woozy but determined to hold his ground, mentally as well as physically, Morgan blinked at the stocky Inupiaq. "I don't follow you."

"Then follow me," Tungarook directed him. "Nobody will believe you anyway." Turning, he headed for a closed door. "Casey is charging the batteries."

"I know. She told me." Morgan tottered after his host. "What has that got to do with …?"

As soon as the door was opened and he followed the shorter man through the intervening boot room, he saw.

The wall of frigid air hit him the instant they stepped out of the changing area and he was tempted to retreat to the warm living room. Brain and body both screamed at him to scurry back to the realm of snug blankets and cozy couch. What he saw, however, held him transfixed. Transfixed and disbelieving. Transfixed and disbelieving and with his hair standing on end. Not in the metaphorical sense, either. Though the longest strands were little more than an inch in extent, each was now standing straight out from the sides and top of his head. Next to him, Albert Tungarook's much longer black hair was also standing stiffly at attention, making him look like a relative to the porcupine.

Two sleek but well-used snow machines dominated the tiny, constricted garage. Like an army of pawns surrounding their king and queen, everything from shovels to neatly-racked snowshoes lined and lay against the insulated metal walls. Armories of tools hung from the interior siding, coils of cable and hose were hooked to the walls like hibernating snakes, drums of gasoline huddled against the far wall like so many herded wombats, and in one corner, splayed pelts stood stacked like shoe leather. A rack of steel shelves welded to the rear wall held wired-together ranks of deep-cycle marine batteries. One tangle of cables ran rightward to resolve itself into the inner wall of the house. A second serpentine confusion emerged from a nearby floor-mounted transformer. A skylight dimpled the roof overhead. At present it was open to the cold and the stars.

Her right arm upraised, fingers extended, Casey Tungarook stood directly beneath the opening. Seemingly unsupported, her long black hair was standing straight up, as if being tugged by the vacuum of space. Dropping straight down from the heavens, a tongue of cold green blaze entered the garage via the open skylight. It coursed down her upthrust arm, through her body, out her outstretched left arm, and into the transformer on which her open palm rested. The expression on her face was perfectly neutral. She was neither smiling nor frowning. Certainly she was not in pain. If anything, an awed Morgan decided, she looked bored.

Seeing him gaping at her, she turned toward him and smiled reassuringly, her brown skin flushed celadon. "It doesn't hurt," she called to him above the soft hiss of the electric heavens that suffused the garage. "Though it does kind of tickle."

Morgan did not respond. He had no idea how to respond. What he was witnessing was so implausible, so physically far-fetched, that he was sure anything he might say would leave him sounding like a complete idiot. In the absence of a response, the girl adjusted her stance slightly. The slender downpour of green fire promptly shifted with her, shimmying like a drapery sewn of translucent satin.

Behind their respective glass windows on the multiplicity of heavy-duty storage batteries, a multitude of individual red needles were steadily advancing from left to right.

Morgan did not realize how long he had been standing in stupefied silence until the chill that had invaded his open mouth began to sting his jaws. He felt Tungarook's hand on his arm.

"Let's go back inside," his host suggested gently. "It's cold in the garage when Casey is working. She'll be finished soon."

"Yes," Morgan heard a voice murmur. His own. "Back inside."

His hands had not trembled when they had taken the mug of hot chocolate from the girl's fingers, but they did now. He did not even try to pick up the cup as he stared across the room at Tungarook.

"I either just saw something impossible," he declared immediately, "or else there's a concealed film crew here making a movie and I just found myself in the middle of a special effect."

His host chuckled. "Yeah, that's what everybody thinks when they see Casey doing her thing."

Morgan blinked. "I'm not the first?"

Tungarook shook his head. "You're the first non-Inupiaq. The others, they accept it. Living up here for ten thousand years or so, people come around to accepting all kinds of things folks from down south would call impossible. We have stories and legends for happenings that have never even occurred to you."

"So it's—magic?" Outside, the green glow had vanished, but Casey did not reappear. Checking her wiring, perhaps. In the truest sense of the term?

"What, are you calling me a superstitious savage?" At the stricken look that appeared on Morgan's face, Tungarook laughed out loud. "Nothing magical about it," he replied, taking pity on his guest. "It's simple physics. Well," he corrected himself, "maybe not so simple. But physics. I've discussed the basis with some of the scientists at the Arctic Research Center outside of town. Without mentioning my daughter's unusual ability, of course. But process and effect. To put it succinctly, Casey can channel the aurora."

Morgan found himself longing for something to drink that was stronger than hot chocolate. "Still sounds like magic to me." He found his gaze being drawn to the door that led toward the garage. "Looked like magic, too."

Tungarook set his mug aside. "What do you know about the aurora borealis?"

"It's pretty." Morgan added apologetically, "I'm just a photographer, most of the time."

"And I'm just a hunter, some of the time," his host replied. "But I have a singular daughter, and I need to know all that I can about her. How *did* you think we kept the batteries charged sufficiently way out here by ourselves to supply all this light and heat?"

"I didn't think about it. As you'll recall," Morgan added wryly, "when I got here I was nearly frozen to death."

"Oh yeah, so you were. Well, the scientists tell me you get an auroral display when charged particles in the Earth's magnetosphere collide with and excite atoms in the upper atmosphere. These atoms get rid of their gained energy in the form of light. Because most of the emissions come from something called atomic oxygen, most auroras have a green or red glow. Nitrogen gives blue and purple. I'm told there's also infrared, ultraviolet, and X-rays, but we don't see those down here." He poured himself a fresh mug of steam and chocolate.

"Casey may be the first person, at least in our time, who can channel the aurora, but she's not the first incident where it has happened. Back in 1859 a monster storm on the sun produced maybe the strongest aurora in your time and mine. Most of the telegraph lines around the world went crazy; in and out of service, because of the auroral discharge. But it turned out that some of the lines were just the right length and orientation to let a—it's called a geomagnetically induced current—flow through them, and allow the lines to be used for normal communication."

Morgan made a face. "Oh, come on now. Not really."

Tungarook nodded. "A couple of operators communicating between Boston and Portland, Oregon switched off their station power and transmitted back and forth for two hours using nothing but auroral current. Said the line worked better on auroral power than it did with their usual batteries." He waved his mug. "When she puts her arms and body just so, Casey can align herself the same way. Maybe her mother took too many iron supplements when she was pregnant. Maybe there was an impurity in them. I don't know. "

Morgan turned contemplative. "Every month there are stories about people conducting lightning through their bodies and into the ground, or into other objects. Then there are the tricks people play with Tesla coils. But I've never heard of anyone channeling the aurora itself."

Lifting his mug to his lips, Tungarook replied absolutely dead-pan. "You should get out more. I could rent you a snow machine."

"Actually, right now, I'm thinking more of the bed in my hotel room back in Barrow. That, and a steak."

"Can't do steak, but have you ever had uhnavik?" Morgan shook his head no. "I'll get some out of the cold box. Whale blubber with the skin still on. Boil it 'til it's soft enough to chew, put on lots of salt. You'll like it. It'll remind you of calamari. Eat first, then sleep. I'll wake you before sun-up."

Morgan had to grin again. "I don't think I'll sleep 'til February." More somberly he added, "What makes you think I won't talk about your daughter and come back here with a news crew?"

"Two things." His genial host spoke confidently. "First, because you couldn't get a news crew or even another photographer out to this place in winter without everybody in Barrow knowing about it first and letting me know in advance. It's too far from Prudhoe or Fairbanks for a helicopter pilot to risk his machine in the dark and the cold and the wind to find one little house on the tundra." For the first time since Morgan had made the hunter's acquaintance, the man's gaze hardened.

"Second, I just saved your life. You owe me big time. So I ask you to keep quiet about this thing, and leave my daughter be. Sure she's got a strange ability, but outside of that she's a normal, regular teen. If word of what she can do gets out, the scientists will be all over her like mosquitoes on a caribou herd in summer. She won't have a life worth anything. If you had a daughter, would you want her likeness and life plastered all over the media, every week, every month, until the day she died?"

"I'm not married," Morgan replied. He remembered the eyes of the wolf, substituted the flash of the media. "It hurts to say yes, but— I've photographed other things and kept them private. I guess I can do the same with this. And you're right—I do owe you."

"Good man." Turning, Tungarook raised his voice. "Hey Casey! The white guy says he'll keep his mouth shut!"

The girl reappeared a moment later. In spite of himself, Morgan could not keep from staring. She looked unchanged, unaffected, utterly average. Had long dead ancestors who possessed her ability once been burned as witches? He could not recall reading anything about the Inupiaq burning or sacrificing people. It was not part of their culture. Every life in the frozen north was too valuable to throw away on such nonsense.

She came toward him, her expression a mixture of youthful shyness and special knowledge. "Thanks, mister. I really don't want to be in the papers. I just want to graduate, get my degree, and have a family. You can't do that if people are studying you like a bug under glass."

Morgan flashed on a sudden, unsettling image of a baby in a

cradle teething quietly on green lightning. "I understand." He eyed her up and down. "It really doesn't hurt?"

She laughed. "Like I said, it just kind of tickles." Her eyes flashed mischievously. "Would you like to see what else I can do?"

Morgan looked uncertain. "Power up a snow machine?"

"Better than that. Let me put on my parka. You come outside."

Outside? He hesitated. He had just barely survived an extended period in a most unfriendly outside. A glance through the window showed that the wind had, at least momentarily, died. And he had not. He looked questioningly over at his host.

"Go on," Tungarook urged him, a twinkle in his eye. "I'll come too, so you won't get lost."

Jibe or joke, it was enough to motivate Morgan. "Where are my clothes?"

The hunter rose from his chair. "On a grill over the stove. Should be nice and warm by now. I'll get them."

The chill outside bit instantly and hard. Morgan had to fight down the urge to rush back into the inviting warmth of the house. The thin layer of ice and snow crunched beneath his boots as he followed Tungarook out through the boot room and then the side door of the garage. That was how you entered and exited the house. In the absence of neighbors a normal front door would have been superfluous, and leaked heat.

In all directions there was nothing to be seen but mostly flat, occasionally bumpy ground. Not a tree, not a bush, not a sprig of grass. The latter would come with the sun and the Spring, both still months away from making an appearance. For now and for weeks ahead there would be nothing but ice, snow, killing wind, the occasional mournful cry of a wolf, and more stars than could be imagined even in Wisconsin. That, and the astonishing light storm that pranced and strut across the sky in rolling, mesmerizing waves of incandescent green and red.

Having donned her parka and boots, Casey joined them. While her father and their guest halted not far from the house, she kept walking until she was a good thirty yards or so away. For what little good it did, Morgan had his arms folded across his chest. He managed to forbear from slapping his sides and jumping up and down. Very soon he was not moving at all, and hardly daring to breathe.

Casey Tungarook had raised both arms toward the sky. Within moments, she was standing within a wavering spire of green radiance so intense it made Morgan blink to look directly at it. Perhaps a little brighter and wider, it was otherwise no different from the phenomenon he had observed in the garage.

Lowering her arms until they were thrust straight out to the sides, she began to spin. Slowly at first, then faster and faster. Occasionally she would leap into the air. Though few Inupiaq had the build of a ballerina, Casey's jumps were often impressive, and visibly enthusiastic.

Leaning close to the enthralled photographer, Tungarook murmured from beneath the wolverine-rimmed hood of his parka. "Our people are great singers and dancers." He smiled anew. "We have lots of time to practice, you know."

Morgan heard but did not turn to look at the hunter. In front of him, out on the rocky snow-swept ground, a single smiling, stocky sixteen-year old was singing a song in her own ancient language, spinning and twirling as she was enveloped in a softly hissing translucent tornado of light that spread farther and farther beyond her outstretched arms, until it seemed that the entire tundra was ablaze with red and green incandescence.

As the shimmering aurora that had been brought to ground expanded to envelop him as well, the smile on the face of a thoroughly entranced Morgan grew wider and wider. There were many things he could have said, innumerable comments he could have made. Instead, like the proud father standing beside him, he said nothing. Merely looked on in rapt silence as the girl before them continued to dance away the arctic night, partnering with the fire from the sky.

7

Pardon Our Conquest

I suppose in some ways this story could be considered a companion piece to "Unvasion." Except that in this instance, as Pogo might say, the aliens is us. When we invaded Iraq, I remember writing that redoubtable international news magazine, The Economist, *a letter to the editor that they printed in which I pointed out that one reason the invasion was a bad idea was because such a war would not be cost-effective.*

Traditional warfare is often self-defeating because the victor as well as the vanquished ends up impoverished by the effort expended. Surely there must be other ways to dominate an opponent that do not require the sacrifice of great treasure and thousands if not millions of lives? A more civilized form of combat, if you will. Gamers engage in it every day, with the only collateral damage usually being to the nearest refrigerator.

If it can be done on-line and on-board, why not in-life?

ADMIRAL GORELKII SHIFTED his seat on the meter-thick, jewel-encrusted, ceremonial golden cushion that rose behind the sweeping transparent arc of the solid crystal crescent moon, and fumed. His ample pale gray bulk was draped in a bloom of multihued embroidered standards, each one representing one of the ancient Great Hordes that together comprised the Empire of the Three Suns. They weighed on him physically as well as historically. The wearing of the standards was a great honor accorded to a select few only on the most extraordinary occasions.

Unfortunately for him, today's extraordinary occasion was one of surrender.

His courage and willingness in accepting the responsibility for heading the disagreeable negotiations was recognized on all five inhabited worlds of the three systems that comprised the Empire. That did not mean he looked forward to the impending ceremony. What the exact details would consist of he did not know. What specific protocol was to be followed he did not know.

No doubt the conquerors of the Empire would be enlightening him in due course.

The Falan had never been a species to hesitate. Imbued with the heady wine of discovery and an assurance of their own superiority, they had looked forward to the steady expansion of their Empire in the direction of the arm of the galaxy that held a greater density of star systems than their own immediate vicinity. Following initial exploration they had discovered, explored, charted, and engaged in the successful colonization of two new habitable systems.

Then they had found Drax IV.

So it was called by the short, multi-legged, hard-carapaced creatures who inhabited the cities and towns they had wrested from its jungles and forests. Mild in temperament, absurd in appearance, they claimed to be part of a vast interstellar dominion called the Commonwealth. Whether this unknown political entity be vast, small, or imaginary, their polite insistence on its existence did nothing to deter the aggressive Falan. It was announced that the system of Drax would be incorporated into the Empire forthwith, and any foolish resistance met with fire and destruction on a planetary scale. Declaring war, the Falan proceeded to open hostilities by unleashing a small example of their firepower on a little-populated corner of the planet.

Subsequent to this ferocious demonstration, the inhabitants requested some time to contemplate their limited alternatives. While any military prowess on their part remained undetermined, they proved expert in the arts of obfuscation and delay. Eventually the patience of the Falan, never extensive to begin with, ran out.

The Falan ultimatum happened to coincide with the arrival of a fleet of fifty Commonwealth warships, which was considerably more than the two dozen or so the Empire could muster. When informed that this was a scouting force sent to determine the precise nature of the threat that had been levied against Drax, and that the main armada of the so-called Commonwealth had not even been assembled, consternation and despair among the Falan was followed by reluctant but unavoidable capitulation.

Gorelkii and his frustrated fellow career officers would have preferred to test the strength of the enemy warships in battle. As for the claim that they represented only a scouting force, such alien assertions could not be verified. They might be composed of nothing more than bluster on the part of the inhabitants of Drax. But Gorelkii and his comrades had been overridden by the Polity of the Three Suns, whose fear of utter annihilation if hostilities commenced and the possibility that those on the newly arrived enemy vessels were telling the truth was a realistic extrapolation based on their own fractious racial history.

"The Falan must be preserved," he had been informed solemnly. "We will build our strength in secret, improve our weapons, advance our science. In time we will throw off the yoke of the enemy and carry the battle to its homeworlds."

Fifty warships, he thought as he sat behind the glittering crescent moon. Scouting force. It was scarce to be believed. When queried, the inhabitants of Drax IV had declined to elaborate on the actual size and extent of their mysterious "Commonwealth." Though not looking forward to negotiating the formal terms of surrender, Gorelkii knew that it would buy the Falan time to learn exactly what they were up against. Building on that knowledge, they would be able to prepare their inevitable unstoppable response.

Adjutant Bardanat entered through the wide, arched entrance of contoured metal. The muscles of his heavy bipedal form bulged beneath his gleaming uniform and his small black eyes glittered beneath a single thrust of projecting bone. One tri-fingered hand snapped ceilingward in salute. His tone was its usual clipped, wholly professional self, save for what Gorelkii took to be a touch of bemusement.

"The diplomatic representatives of the Commonwealth are here, Grand Admiral." Bardanat hesitated and his voice lost some of its formal stress. "They are ... they are ..."

"Well, pour it out, Adjutant! *What* are they?"

Bardanat's fleshy eyefolds contracted in his species' equivalent of a blink. "Not what I expected, Admiral."

Gorelkii snorted through the single large respiratory opening set high in the center of his chest and below his thick neck. The nostril was framed by ribbons of valor that had been permanently encased in gleaming protective transparencies. The color tint of each transparency indicated the level of accomplishment that accented each ribbon.

"It doesn't matter what you expected, or I. We must deal with them." He gestured with a powerful, double-jointed arm. "Admit them."

He readied himself. Though his people had been defeated without a shot having been fired, a missile being unleashed, or an energy beam deployed, he would attempt to bargain as an equal. The Admiral could rant and rave with the most voluble politician. He could be out-argued, but he could not be intimidated. It was one of the reasons he had been chosen to head the negotiations. It was universally conceded among the Polity that no one in the Empire was likely to obtain better terms than Grand Admiral Gorelkii.

Steeping to the left, Adjutant Bardanat assumed a position of ready respect. Legs contracted, upper body straight and stiff, eyes forward, he would hold that position until his muscles screamed for relief or Gorelkii directed him to stand down.

Two shapes were approaching from the far end of the formal antechamber, walking toward him from the towering main entry arch. Gorelkii could not keep from tensing. What would they demand? How would they treat him personally? What kind of confrontational species had the resources to send forth a force of fifty warships merely to scout a confrontation?

When at last the pair finally halted before the curve of the crescent moon, he was shocked by their size. The spindly, big-eyed one he knew from images sent back from Drax. Presently standing on four limbs with another four upraised, it inclined feathery antennae in his direction. A bright blue-green in color, it looked fragile and harmless.

Though bipedal like the Falan, the creature standing beside the thranx appeared even less threatening. So soft and spongy was it that one could actually see bits of its exposed flesh still moving after it had come to a stop. A strange white growth emerged from the top of its skull and also covered much of the lower half of its face. It would take little effort, Gorelkii thought, to crush them both, splintering the thranx-thing and pounding its taller companion to a pulp.

Should he give in to the natural impulse, however, he knew it would put something of a damper on the forthcoming negotiations. He forced down his instinctive feelings and kept his massive three-fingered hands locked together in front of him.

Lumbering forward, Bardanat checked to make sure the translator positioned in front of his cutting teeth was operational before he began to declaim forcefully without looking to left or right. "I present to you Grand Admiral Gorelkii-vant, Destroyer of Worlds, Sovereign of the Nation-Clan Hasekar, Supreme Commander of the First Fleet Majestic, Defender of Empire, Scion of the Second Sun!"

His soft mouth parting to reveal tiny white teeth behind his own hair-thin translation device, the white-crowned biped stepped forward and thrust a limb across the crystal arc in Gorelkii's direction, causing the Admiral to briefly recoil. "Hi, I'm Bill. William Chen-Khamsa, but my friends all call me Bill." Gesturing at his hard-shelled companion, he added, "That's the Eint Colvinyarev. He's from Hivehom and I'm from Earth."

Scuttling sideways, Adjutant Bardanat leaned slightly toward his commander and whispered. "The extended limb of the human creature, Grand Admiral. I believe you are supposed to make contact with the end."

Baffled but adaptive, Gorelkii reached out with a massive hand. Unable with his more numerous but much smaller fingers to envelop it all, the human creature took two of the three thick proffered fingers and shook them up and down several times. Releasing its lightweight but assured grasp, it then stepped back.

"Pleased to meet you, Admiral." Gesturing with its head, the being indicated Gorelkii's expansive torso. "Are those awards on your chest? I don't know their individual significance, of course, but even a visitor like myself can see that they're very striking!"

Flattery as an opening ploy, Gorelkii told himself. Somewhat unex-pected, given that he was the supine party. He would not succumb to it of course. Still, there was no harm in utilizing his personal history to make an impact on this unimposing pair. He proceeded to do so.

When he had finished, the thranx dipped its head and antennae low in his direction. "Most impressive! I can see that the Polity of the Three Suns chose from among the best of your kind to represent them."

"The Polity makes no mistakes!" Gorelkii's voice reverberated through the vaulted, effusively decorated audience chamber. "Though we have surrendered to your forces, we have not been defeated, as no actual combat has taken place."

"We agree absolutely." Though massing far less than the average Falan, the human's eyes were the same size. The Bill's were blue, a color that fascinated Gorelkii. All Falan eyes were black or shades of very dark gray. "We consider ourselves fortunate to have escaped your wrath."

Intriguing though the ocular diversion was, Gorelkii ceased musing on the startlingly bright color of alien eyes. "Excuse me?"

"Clearly after learning more about you and your kind, any conflict between our three species would have resulted in terrible losses on our side. We would have been devastated! We are so very grateful that you have deigned to refrain from destroying us."

"Yes, *ccr!lk.*" Folding its forelegs beneath its abdomen, the thranx executed a deep bow. "Gratitude compels us to abase ourselves before you."

What was going on here? Gorelkii thought confusedly. What kind of game were these representatives playing at? He bemoaned his ignorance of the culture of the triumphant species. He did not know enough to recognize if he was being mocked. In the absence of such data he could only improvise his responses.

"Yes—well, the casualties the combined fleets would have wreaked on your forces would have been terrible!"

"Truly, we are aware." The thranx rose out of its forward-inclining stance to regard the Admiral with golden compound eyes. "It is out of this awe and respect that we most cordially invite you to bring the Empire of the Three Suns into the Commonwealth."

Ah, there it was, at last! Gorelkii told himself with satisfaction. Couched in respectful, almost deferential terms, but unmistakable none the less. On familiar rhetorical ground once again, he immediately challenged.

"You propose to absorb us into your own federation! Well I can tell you, both as an Admiral of the Falan and as … !"

"No, no, you've got it all wrong!" So absurd a picture did the human present, with its waving little arms and wide eyes, that Gorelkii did not take exception to the clumsy interruption. "Colvinyarev speaks honestly when he says it's an invitation. If it so wishes, the Empire can go on its happy way with as little or as much contact with the Commonwealth as it desires. There is no compulsion of any kind to participate."

The thranx gestured first-degree concurrence, though the elaborate gesticulations of foothands and truhands meant nothing to the Admiral. "Many intelligent species besides our own are members of the Commonwealth. Some in full, some only in part. The only thing we have in absolute common is sentience. Several participate actively in decisions of Commonwealth policy, others tend to their own world or worlds and leave policy making to the rest." A small truhand gestured. "The Falan would surely rank among the most imposing species ever to join."

Despite the resolve with which he had determined to enter into the negotiations, Gorelkii found himself slightly dazed. Nothing was proceeding as expected. He resolved to force matters back onto a familiar keel.

"It is for the Polity and not I to consider such topics. I sit before you only to settle formal matters of surrender." He leaned forward, his massive bulk greater than that of human and thranx combined, his jet-black eyes glittering challengingly. "First we will dispose of the matter of reparations…."

Human and thranx looked at one another. "What reparations?" The human turned back to face the Admiral. "A couple of your ships inflicted some minor damage on Drax IV. Nothing that can't be fixed. Forget about it. What's a little petty devastation between friends?"

Once again Gorelkii's eyepads performed the Falan blink. "No reparations?"

The human showed its teeth again. "No reparations."

"Very well then." The Admiral drew himself up. "We will proceed to the highly sensitive matter of disarmament, which I assure you the Polity will regard with the most …"

This time it was the thranx who broke in. "You can keep and maintain all of your warships."

"*All* of them?" the Adjutant blurted. "All three fleets?" It was an outrageous breach of protocol, but Gorelkii could hardly chastise Bardanat for speaking out. The Admiral was equally shocked by the visitors' response.

"Well, of course," the human replied cheerfully. "They're *your* ships, after all."

"Restriction of movement, then." Recovering, Gorelkii cast a warning look in Bardanat's direction to remind the Adjutant who and where he was.

"No restrictions." Instead of meeting the Admiral's eyes, the human was leaning forward to examine the arc of the crescent moon. "This is really beautiful workmanship. I can't find a single flaw or inclusion. I know that the crafts folk who fashioned it would find ready acceptance of their work on many worlds of the Commonwealth." He blinked once. "As I said, they're your ships."

Gorelkii's thoughts were awhirl. "Commonwealth military garrisons on the five worlds. How extensive?"

The human looked again at his thranx companion. "Why would we want to establish a military presence on any of your worlds? You're not part of the Commonwealth. Not yet, anyway."

"But," the thranx added, "we would be flattered if you would situate some of your forces—completely independent, of course—on several of our worlds. Given the impression the Falan have made on the peoples of the Commonwealth, I'm certain their presence would be both welcome and admired."

"Wait ..." Gorelkii struggled to gather himself. "You want *us* to establish a military presence on some of *your* worlds?"

The human's head bobbed lightly up and down. "Would you do us that honor?"

Honor. No reparations. No disarmament. Everything the two representatives had said so far was suggestive of craven cowardice. Or ...?

Gorelkii was a soldier. He knew how to fight. He even knew how to surrender. His long and distinguished career had prepared him for both eventualities. But nothing he had experienced or studied had prepared him for negotiations like this.

"I am sure," he said quickly, "that the Polity would be most pleased to place representatives of the Empire's military on as many of your worlds as would be allowed."

"Excellent!" As far as Gorelkii could ascertain, the human's expression of delight was sincere. "We would be pleased to engage in cultural and commercial exchanges as well. According to whatever procedures and restrictions your government decides to impose, of course."

"Yes, well, as I have already mentioned, I am not empowered to negotiate such matters."

The human's head moved again, the white growth covering part of his face bobbing with the movement. "I'm positive others can work out the details." He looked to his colleague. "I think that's about it, Col."

"Yes," the thranx agreed. He eyed the Admiral. "Is there anything else you would like to discuss, your excellency? If you have the time, we would be flattered to invite you to a reception to be given aboard our ship, currently in stationary orbit above this city. You may of course bring with you any relations or friends that you would like. As our food synthesizers are programmed to satisfy the nutritional requirements of many species, I am sure they can create victuals that you would find of culinary interest, *srral!k.*"

Gorelkii hesitated. The negotiations had gone well. No, amazingly well. Far, far better than even the most pessimistic member of the Polity could have imagined. He considered the thranx's offer. Refusing an invitation might be construed as an affront. It would be foolish to risk all that had been attained over such a slight request. Besides which he could not deny holding a personal interest in learning as much as he could about these obscenely deferential creatures.

"I accept your invitation." He indicated the stiff-legged Bardanat. "My Adjutant will handle the details. But I warn you," he added threateningly, "the details of these proceedings have been exhaustively recorded by multiple concealed sources. Any attempt at a future date to alter the terms of surrender will be met with …!"

The visitors' penchant for interruption struck yet again. "Oh, let's not call it that," the human insisted. "'Surrender' is such an unsociable term. I believe the official documents to be agreed upon are titled 'Instruments of Eternal and Lasting Friendship between the

Commonwealth of the Humanx and the Grand and Indivisible Empire of the Three Suns.' They are already being communicated to your Polity for formal final review and execution."

Gorelkii tapped his translator. In the course of negotiations he had fully expected to hear the term "execution" employed, but before now, and not in relation to bureaucratic formalities.

"We do have one last request." The human was eyeing him thoughtfully.

Here it comes, Gorelkii thought. He steeled himself for whatever last-minute ultimate demand might be forthcoming. "Which is?"

Raising a spindly arm, the white-haired human pointed at the Admiral. "Would you wear that magnificent uniform, or whatever you call your current spectacular attire, when you attend our reception? I know that all of our military as well as diplomatic people will be as impressed by it as Col and I have been."

Gorelkii found himself gesturing automatically. "Yes. Yes, that can be arranged."

"Splendid!" Stepping forward, the human extended his arm once more. This time Gorelkii knew how to respond. They shook hands, gray enveloping beige. As the alien biped retreated, his thranx colleague advanced, dipped his head, and brushed the Admiral's still extended trio of fingers with his antennae. The contact was negligible.

"We are most grateful for your hospitality," the hard-shell murmured. "I personally look forward to greeting and entertaining you and your companions on board our vessel."

Gorelkii sat in silence for a long time after the two Commonwealth diplomats had departed. Only an involuntary and irrepressible grunt of pain from Bardanat reminded the Admiral that his Adjutant was still locked in the ritual pose of Formal Reception.

"Straighten," he told Bardanat.

"Gratitude, Admiral." The Adjutant was relieved. "I …" He hesitated, then asked the question that he could not suppress. "It is not for me to determine, but from what I was witness to I am presuming that according to the hopes and expectations of the Polity and of your personal self, the negotiations went well enough?"

"You may presume correctly, Adjutant." Gorelkii was gazing down the arched Corridor of Mortality through which the diplomats had taken their leave. "There's just one thing of which I remain uncertain."

Bardanat stared back at the Grand Admiral, Destroyer of Worlds, etc. "What is that, Excellency?"

Gorelkii looked over at him. "Remind me again: this war. We lost—didn't we?"

$$8$$

That Creeping Sensation

3 50 million years ago. Or 300 million years ago. What's fifty million years when you're talking about giant bugs?

It's the Carboniferous period, when oversized arthropods ruled the Earth. Most folks think of it as hot and humid, which it was. Fewer realize that there was a lot more oxygen in the atmosphere. More oxygen allows insects, who have an entirely different and generally less efficient respiratory system than mammals and reptiles and a number of other life forms, to grow larger. How much larger? Naw ... I'm not going to do that work for you. If you're curious to read how big the Protodonata *and their fellow carboniferans grew, there's plenty to read about them.*

Doing so got me to wondering what might happen to their descendents if the oxygen level in our atmosphere rose suddenly and significantly once again. Thanks to our own ignorance....

"CODE FOUR, CODE FOUR!"

Sgt. Lissa-Marie nodded to her partner and Corporal Gustafson acknowledged the alarm. It was the fourth Code Four of what had long since turned into a long hot one—both temperature-wise and professionally. She checked a floating readout: it declared that the temperature outside the sealed, climate-controlled truck cab was ninety-six degrees Fahrenheit at two in the afternoon. Happily the humidity was unusually low, floating right around the eighty percent mark.

"Gun it," she growled. From behind the wheel Gustafson nodded and floored the accelerator. Supplying instant torque, the electric motors mounted above each of the panel truck's four wheels sent it leaping forward. As the sharp acceleration shoved her back into her seat she directed her voice to the omnidirectional pickup mounted in the roof.

"What is it this time?"

"Bees." The human dispatcher's reply was as terse as it was meaningful. "Nobody dead, but two teens on their way to Metro Emergency."

"They're getting smarter." Gustafson chewed his lower lip as he concentrated on his driving.

"Manure," she shot back. "You're anthropomorphizing. That's dangerous in work like ours."

Her younger subordinate shook his head as much as his tightly contoured seat would allow. "It's true." He refused to drop the contention. "They're getting smarter. You can sense it. You can see it. They don't just crawl around and wait to be smoked anymore. They react earlier. They're ...," he glanced over at her, "they're anticipating."

She shrugged and returned her gaze forward, out the armored windshield. "Just drive. If you insist, we can continue with your insane speculations after we've finished the job."

The streets of Atlanta's outer ring were nearly deserted. Few people chose to spend money on an expensive personal vehicle anymore. Not when public transportation was so much cheaper and a steady stream of workers kept the rails and tunnels free of the insects that obscured windshields and clogged wheel wells after barely twenty minutes of driving. The lack of traffic certainly made things easier for the exterminator branch of the military to which the two people in the truck belonged. Lissa was musing on the vilm she had been reading when a sudden swerve by Gustafson caused her to lurch and curse. Her partner was apologetic.

"Sorry. Roaches," he explained.

She nodded her understanding and relaxed anew. One three-foot roach wouldn't damage the specially armored truck, but if they'd hit

the arthropod head on they would have had to explain their careless-
ness to the cleanup crew back at base.

As they neared their destination she lifted her reducer off its hook
and made sure it fit snuggly over her nose and mouth. Like everyone
else she hated having to wear the damn thing. No matter how much
they improved and miniaturized the integrated cooling system, you
still sweated twice as much behind the device. But it was necessary. It
wouldn't do to consistently suck air that was nearly forty percent
oxygen and still rising. That might have been tolerable if the runaway
atmosphere hadn't also grown hotter and markedly more humid.

At least she'd never been in a fire, she told herself. Like most
people she shuddered at the thought. Given the current concentration
of oxygen in the atmosphere, the smallest fire tended to erupt into an
inferno in no time. *Leave those worries to the fire brigades,* she told herself.
The multinational she worked for had enough to do trying to keep
ahead of the bugs.

As studies of the Carboniferous Era, the climate in Earth's history
nearest to that of the present day, had shown, the higher the oxygen
content of the air, the bigger bugs could grow. Mankind's loathing of
the arthropods with whom he was compelled to share the planet had
increased proportionately.

"We're here." Gustafson brought the truck to a halt outside the
single-family home.

They didn't have to look for the bees. They were all over the one-
story residence they intended to appropriate. A cluster of civilian
emergency vehicles was drawn up nearby. Occasionally a crack would
sound from one of the tightly-sealed police cruisers and a six-inch bee
would go down, obliterated by a blast of micro bugshot. Operating in
such piecemeal fashion the cops could deal with the bees, but only by
expending a lot of expensive ammunition and at the cost of causing
serious collateral damage to the immediate neighborhood. Buttoned-
up in their cruisers and guarding the perimeter they had established
around the home, they had hunkered down to await the arrival of
military specialists.

That would be me and Gustafson, she knew.

Already half dressed for the extirpation, she wiggled around in the
truck cab as she donned the rest of her suit. An ancient apiarist would
have looked on in amazement as she zipped up the one-piece rein-

forced Kevlar suit, armorglass helmet, and metalized boots. Once dressed, individual cooling systems were double-checked. Ten minutes trapped inside one of the sealed suits in the current heat and humidity would bring even a fit person down. The coolers were absolutely necessary, as were the tanks of poison spray the two exterminators affixed to their back plates. When each had concluded preparations, they took care to check the seals of one other's suit. A few stings from the six-inch long bees contained more than enough venom to kill.

"Let's go," she murmured. Gustafson shot her a look, nodded, and cracked the driver's-side door.

The bees pounced on them immediately. Exhibiting a determination and aggression unknown to their smaller ancestors, several dozen of them assailed the two bipedal figures that had started toward the house. The swarm covered that edifice entirely. From decorative chimney to broken windows it was blanketed by a heaving, throbbing, humming scrum of giant bees. Lissa grunted as one bee after another dove to fruitlessly slam its stinger into her impenetrable suit. Walking toward the house through such a persistent swarm was like stumbling around a boxing ring with your opponent allowed to hit you from any and every angle. And your opponent was an octopus.

As they reached the front of the overrun house a nervous voice sounded on an open police channel on Lissa's helmet communicator.

"We think the Queen's around back, near the swimming pool."

"Thanks." She didn't have to relay the information to Gustafson. The Corporal had picked up the same transmission.

Working their way around to the back they found the swarm there even thicker than what they had encountered out front. Surrounded by increasingly agitated workers, the Queen had settled herself against a corner of the house where workers were already preparing hexagonal wax tubes to receive the first eggs. She never got the chance to lay them.

"You know the routine." Lissa muttered into her helmet pickup. "Start with the Queen, work back to front."

Holding his sprayer, her partner nodded even as he opened fire.

The killing mist that would render the house uninhabitable began to send bees tumbling off the walls, roof, and one another. Most staggered drunkenly for a few seconds before collapsing in small black and orange heaps. Lissa kicked accumulating piles of plump, boldly striped bodies aside as she and Gustafson finished up in the back yard and started working their way around to the front.

"Ware ten o'clock!" she yelled as she raised the muzzle of her sprayer.

The trio of foot-long yellow jackets, however, were only interested in taking a few of the now panicky live bees. Natural predators of such hives, they were the human's allies in extirpation. Though even more formidable than the giant honeybees, they had no interest in the two suited humans. Which was a good thing, Lissa knew. A yellowjacket's stinger could punch into an unprotected human like a stiletto.

As she and the Corporal worked their way through the swarm she reflected on the unexpected turn of history. When the Greenhouse Effect had begun to set in, scientists had worried about the presumed surplus of carbon dioxide that was expected to result. They had failed to account for Earth's astonishing ability to adapt to even fast-changing circumstances.

With the increased heat and humidity, plant life had gone berserk. Rainforests like those of the Amazon and Congo that had once been under threat expanded outward. Loggers intent on cutting down the big, old trees paid no attention to the fecund explosion of ferns, cycads, and soft-bodied plants that flourished in their wake. A serious problem in temperate times, vines and creepers like the ubiquitous kudzu experienced rates of growth approaching the exponential.

The great sucking sound which resulted was that of new vegetation taking carbon dioxide out of the atmosphere and dumping oxygen in its wake. Their size restricted for eons by the inability of their primitive respiratory systems to extract enough oxygen from the atmosphere, arthropods responded to the new oxy-rich air by growing to sizes not seen since similar conditions existed more than 300 million years ago. Short-lived species were the first to adapt, with each new generation growing a little larger than its predecessor as it feasted on the increasingly oxygen-rich atmosphere.

There had been no bees in the Carboniferous, she knew, because there had been no flowers. But modern plants had adapted to the radical climate change as eagerly as their more primitive ancestors. The result was fewer and increasingly less manageable beehives as bigger bees crowded out smaller competitors.

Changes occurred with such startling rapidity that, in little over a hundred years insects, spiders, and their relatives had not only matched but in some cases surpassed the dimensions attained by their ancient relatives. This made for an increasingly uncomfortable co-existence with the supposedly still dominant simian species on the planet, but a very good living for Lissa and her hastily constituted branch of the military. Nearing fifty, she could remember when her company, one of many that had appeared in the wake of the Runaway, had been able to offer its enlisted personnel predictable hours and regular furloughs. Such downtime still existed, of course, but she was making so much combat pay that she felt unable to turn down the assignments that came her way.

Sure enough, scarcely moments after they had finished their work and a pair of city front-loaders had begun the odious task of scooping up the thousands of dead bee bodies, the truck's com whistled for attention.

"We got a 42B." Gustafson had removed his reducer and was leaning out the open door. The oxygen-dense air might be hazardous for long-term breathing, but it was great for making a quick recovery after a bit of heavy physical exertion. One just had to be careful not to rely on it too long. "Boy stepping on scorpion."

She shook her head as she approached the truck. "That's 42A. 42B is scorpion stepping on boy."

Fortunately, the yard-long arthropod they trapped and killed half an hour later in the public playground hadn't stung anyone. Nocturnal by nature, it had been disturbed by children who had been building a fort. They stood around and watched wide-eyed as the two exterminators hauled the chelatinous carcass away. The scorpion wasn't such a big stretch, Lissa knew. Nine-inch long predecessors had thrived in equatorial rainforests as recently as the twenty-first century. It hadn't taken much of an oxygen boost to grow them to their present frightening size.

They were finishing coffee when the code two red call came in. Looks were exchanged in lieu of words. It was one call neither of them wanted to answer. As senior operative, it fell to Lissa.

"Why us?" She spoke tersely into her tiny mouth pickup. "We've been hot on it all morning."

"Everyone's been hot on it all morning." The dispatcher on duty at the Atlanta Metropolitan Command Center sounded tired. He would not be moved, Lissa knew. "You're the best, sergeant sweetheart. Take care of this one and I'll let you and your buddy break for the rest of the day."

She looked over at Corporal Gustafson, who was hearing the same broadcast. Inside the sealed restaurant equipped with its own industrial-strength reducers they had no need for their face masks. She checked her chronometer. If they wrapped up the call early they would each gain a couple of hours of paid free time.

"All right." She was grumbling as she rose from the table. Other patrons regarded the two uniformed specialists with the respect due their unpleasant and dangerous calling. "But not because you called me the best, Lieutenant. Because you called me sweetheart."

"Don't let it go to your head," the officer finished. "Take care on this one."

A single descendant of *Meganeura* shadowed their truck as they sped through the city streets and out into the suburbs. Since this was an emergency call they had their lights and sirens on, but these didn't dissuade the dragonfly. Its four-foot wingspan flashed iridescent in the heavy, humid air until, finally bored with riding in the truck's airflow, it flashed off toward a nearby office building. Going after a goliath fly, Lissa mused as she let Gustafson focus on his driving. Or one of the city's rapidly diminishing and badly overmatched population of pigeons. Unable to compete with the increasingly large and powerful insects, birds had suffered more than any other group under the Runaway.

The family that had put in the emergency call were grateful for the arrival of the exterminator team, but refused to emerge from the house's safe room where they had taken refuge.

"It's in the basement." On the small heads-up display that floated in front of Lissa's face, the mother looked utterly terrified. So did the two children huddled behind her. "We've had break-ins before. Ants mostly, when they can get across the electrical barrier, and roaches my son can handle with his baseball bat. But this is a first for us."

"Take it easy, ma'am. We're on it."

Looking none too reassured, the woman nodded as the transmission ended. Lissa checked her gear and made sure her reducer was sealed against her face before nodding at Gustafson.

"This'll be your first time dealing with a chilopoda, won't it?" Her partner nodded slowly. "Watch your chest. They always go for the chest."

Donning helmets, they exited the car and headed for the single-family home. No sprays this time. Not for this afternoon's quarry. Both of them hefted pump guns.

The front door had been left open, not to greet the arriving exterminators but in the forlorn hope that the invader might depart of its own volition. Not much chance of that, Lissa knew. Chilopoda favored surroundings that were dark and damp. Eying the family compound and the looming, nearby trees, she sighed. If people were going to live in the woods in this day and age …

As they entered the basement the house's proximity lights flicked on. A good sign. It meant that their quarry wasn't moving. Gun barrel held parallel to the floor, she was first down the stairs. The basement was filled with the usual inconsequential detritus of single-family living: crates of goods meant to be given away that would remain in place forever, a couple of old electric bikes, lawn furniture, the home O2 reducer that allowed residents to move freely about the sealed building without having to don face masks, heavy-duty gardening gear, and more.

A sound made her raise her left hand sharply in warning. Whispering into her mask, she pointed toward a far, unilluminated corner. Gustafson nodded and, without waiting, started toward it.

"I'll take care of it, Lissa. You just …"

"No! Flanking movement or …!"

Too late.

The six-foot long centipede burst from its hiding place to leap straight at her startled companion. Its modern Amazonian ancestors had jumped into the air to catch and feed on bats. This oxygen-charged contemporary monster had no difficulty getting high enough off the ground to go straight for Gustafson's throat. If it got its powerful mandibles into his neck above his shirt and below his helmet and started probing with the poison claws that protruded from its back end …

She raised her gun and fired without thinking.

Guts and goo sprayed everywhere as the pumper blew the monster in two. Still it wasn't finished. As both halves twitched and jerked independently, she approached them with care. Two more shots shattered first the dangerous anterior claws and then the head containing the powerful, snapping mandibles.

Turning, she found her partner on the ground, seated against a trunk while holding his weapon and staring. Walking over to him, she bent slightly as she extended a hand to help him up.

"I ..." he didn't look at her, "I'm sorry, Lissa. It came out so fast that I ..."

She cut him off curtly. "Forget it. First encounter with a chilopoda, no need for excuses."

He stared at her. "You warned me. You said they were fast. The class manual talks about their quickness. But I didn't ..." His voice trailed away.

She gave him a reassuring pat on the back. "Like I said, forget it. Visuals and words in a manual are one thing. Having it jump you in a basement is a little different. They make a tiger seem slow and an insurgent unarmed. Next time you'll be ready."

He nodded somberly, and they climbed the stairs. The basement was a mess, but that was a task for a city or private cleanup crew. Back in the truck she kept expecting to be assigned another job as soon as they reported in that they had successfully completed this one. Surprisingly, the officer on duty seemed inclined to keep his word. The bugband stayed silent.

As a chastened Gustafson headed the truck back toward the military base on the outskirts of the city she leaned forward to have a look at the sky through the windshield. Overcast, as always. The usual tepid rain on tap for the evening. Other than that the weather report was promising. Temperatures in the low nineties and humidity down to seventy-five percent. Things were a lot worse the closer one got to the now nearly uninhabitable tropics, she knew. The tech journals were full of reports of new threats emerging from the depths of the impenetrable Amazon. Ten-foot carnivorous beetles. Deadlier scorpions. Six-inch long fire ants ...

Home and business owners might fret over giant centipedes and spiders with three-foot leg spans, but as a military-trained specialist she worried far more about the ants. All ants. Not because they were prolific and not because they could bite and sting, but because they cooperated. Cooperation could lead to bigger problems than any sting. In terms of sheer numbers, the ants had always been the most successful species on the planet. Let them acquire a little of the always paranoid Gustafson's hypothetical intelligence to go with their new size and …

She checked the weather a last time. Atmospheric oxygen was up to forty-one percent give or take a few decimals. It was continuing its steady rise, as it had over the preceding decades. How big would the bugs get if it reached forty-five percent? Or fifty? How would the fire brigades cope with the increasingly ferocious firestorms that had made wooden building construction a relic of the past?

Rolling down her window she removed her mask and stuck her head out into the lugubrious wind. Gustafson gave her a look but said nothing, focused on his driving. Overhead and unseen, another giant dragonfly dropped lower, sized up the potential prey, and shot away. A human was still too big for it to take down. But if its kind kept growing …

Lissa inhaled deeply of the thick, moist air. It filled her lungs, the oxygen boost reinvigorating her after the confrontation in the basement. Drink of it too much and she would start feeling giddy. There were benefits to the increased oxygen concentration. Athletes, at least while performing in air-conditioned venues, had accomplished remarkable feats. Humanity was adapting to the changed climate. It had always done so. It would continue to do so. And in a radically changed North America, at least, the military would ensure that it would be able to do so.

As an exterminator non-com charged with keeping her city safe, her only fear was that something else just might be adapting a little faster.

9

Rural Singularity

Country folk often tend to come off badly in science-fiction stories that actually deal with science. They're often portrayed as ignorant rubes or used for comic relief. Exceptions would be much of the work of Clifford Simak, who is not as well-known as he ought to be today. I've had the opportunity to interact with a lot of what we would call country folk, both in this country and elsewhere. What they tend to lack is education. But not necessarily inspiration.

There are always exceptions to preconceived notions. And they can be found in the darndest places....

GILCREASE MOPPED his brow with the halfway clean rag he had scrounged from the trunk of the car. The only extant war between New Mexico and Texas was between ranchers and oilmen who each claimed that their side of the border was the one that was hottest in mid-August. Having driven all the way from Albuquerque, Gilcrease was happy to call it a tie and offer a plague on both their hothouses.

Not that it wasn't warm in Albuquerque this time of year, too. It was just that everything seemed hotter in the greater desolation that lay to the east of the Sacramento foothills. This was country that made the high desert terrain around Albuquerque seem positively arctic. With every passing moment he looked forward to the return drive and his nice, cool cubby in the newspaper office.

This was a fool's errand for a slow day, he knew. "Human interest," these occasional excursions into the creases of an anomalous body politic were called. Just his luck to be nominated to do the follow-up on this one.

His first glimpse of the Parkers' "ranch" did not inspire confidence. Furnished in half twenty-first, half nineteenth-century fashion, the single-story rock and wood structure scrunched back against a succession of rising rounded granite hillocks like a bear scratching its ass. There was a windmill that on a good day supplied water to the dwelling. Behind and off to the left side of the house was a traditional barn belted by wooden timbers designed to restrain more cattle than ever roamed this particular homestead.

When Gilcrease drove up in a cloud of dust and muttered adjectives, Walt Parker was working under the hood of that undying icon of mobile American steel known as a full-size pickup truck. With the heavy hood raised it looked as if the truck was saying "ahhh." Parking nearby, the reporter took one last optimistic rag-swipe at his forehead and climbed out. The "keep off the grass" sign posted in the dirt driveway made him smile. The only grass for many miles around was to be found high up in the mountains behind the house.

"Walter Parker? I'm Pat Gilcrease, from the Albuquerque Journal."

Weather-beaten and bank-battered, Parker looked ten years older than the fifty-one to which he would admit. There was more oil in the old towel he was using to clean his hands than in the dusty ground beneath his feet. Gilcrease winced slightly when the man extended a welcoming hand, but seeing no choice he took the greasy fingers firmly. Parker squinted up at the taller, younger man.

"You're here about the two-headed chickens, I expect."

Gilcrease nodded, then found himself frowning. "You have more than one?"

"Whole flock." The rancher shook his head. "People. You show them something you're proud of, tell them to keep it to themselves, and they promptly go and call the media." He shook his head regretfully. "Well, you're here, and you've come all the way from the city, so I expect it would be impolite not to show you."

Gilcrease didn't even take out his camera as the rancher guided his visitor around the house and toward the barn. Between the two stood an enclosure fashioned from wood posts and chicken-wire fencing.

Gilcrease prepared himself for the worst. More than likely he would be shown a badly stitched-and-sewn fake. If he was lucky, one of the rancher's birds might have hatched an authentic mutation. One realistic enough to justify a quick snapshot or two and a short article for the People section of the paper. It really had been a slow news week.

"Here 'tis." Parker unlatched the door to the coop. As he did so, twenty or more clucking chickens came running. They were accompanied by a snowstorm of at least twice as many chicks. Gilcrease eyed them, and his jaw promptly dropped.

Every one of them had two heads. Every one. And they looked as healthy as any comparable flock of normal chickens.

Having anticipated his guest's reaction, Parker was grinning. "Didn't believe, did you, Mr. Gilcrease?"

Having finally succeeded in fumbling his camera out of its pouch, the flabbergasted reporter was snapping pictures like mad. "How— I've seen pictures of two-headed animals before. But it's always only one or two individuals at a time. A two-headed snake, or a two-headed turtle. Even a two-headed sheep. But this ..." Holding the camera in one hand he gestured with the other. "How did this happen?"

"Want to see something else interesting?" A grinning Parker raised a hand. "Wait here."

Gilcrease continued to fire off shots while his host disappeared into the long, low henhouse. When the rancher returned he was holding several eggs. Double-shelled eggs, like perfect little white dumbbells. He handed one to the dumbfounded reporter.

"That's how you get two-headed chickens. You get them to lay double eggs." Like light behind a t-shirt, pride began to show through his initial reticence. "My daughter Suzie bred them."

"Your daughter?"

Parker nodded. "She's one clever little girl. Special." His expression faded somewhat. "You know: 'special.' Home-schooled. Has to be."

Staring at the back of his camera, Gilcrease was reviewing the pictures he had just taken. They were as real as the two-headed chicks presently peep-peeping around his ankles.

"Why is that?" he asked absently, his present attention more focused on the pictures.

"She's addled. Clever, but addled. When she was a lot younger—

eleven, I think she was—we took her to see a doctor in El Paso. Specialist. He examined her, did some tests. Said she was what you call an idiot savant. I was gonna punch the guy out until my wife told me what that meant. My wife's the smart one in the family, Mary is. Visiting her mother in Amarillo this week. She wouldn't like it if she knew there was a reporter out here learning about Suzie. But after the neighbors called your paper …" He shrugged. "I thought it better to come clean about the chickens to a real paper than wait for some tabloid free-lancer to come snooping around."

"I'm flattered. My paper is flattered, I mean." Gilcrease holstered his camera. He had his pictures and his article, but still … "Could I meet your daughter? I promise I won't take any photos without your permission and a signed release. Anything else would be an invasion of privacy."

Parker scrutinized his visitor closely. "You seem like a pretty straight guy, Pat. All right, you can say hi. But be careful what you say and how you say it. Keep things—you know. Simple. And don't touch anything. Especially her toys." Gilcrease nodded.

Parker led him out of the coop and into the barn. It was a spacious construction. Ranch equipment was scattered everywhere. All of it looked well-used. Two of the horse stalls were occupied and one of the occupants neighed inquisitively at their approach. Seeing that both animals had only one head apiece, Gilcrease was mildly disappointed. A quick scan of his surroundings revealed nothing out of the ordinary.

"Suzie's in back," Parker told him. "We fixed up a little playroom and workshop for her. It's where she spends most of her time, puttering around." Near the rear of the barn they halted outside a closed door and his tone darkened. "Promise now: no pictures." Gilcrease reaffirmed his earlier commitment whereupon his host opened the door.

The interior of the corner room was flooded with light from multiple double-paned windows. Surprisingly, there was also a skylight. More surprisingly, the light from both sources fell upon what looked like several folds of dark purple, foot-wide wrapping ribbon suspended in mid-air. At the center of the winding ribbons several yard-long coils of copper wire protruded from the top of a metal ovoid. Cables from the ovoid led to a bank of batteries. The entire setup emitted a very faint hum.

"Amplified solar generator." Parker spoke as though it was the most natural thing in the world. "Another of Suzie's putterings." He jerked a thumb toward the front of the property. "We got another one powers the whole house."

Gilcrease swallowed. His camera was burning a hole in its pouch, but he had promised. "Another one? The same size?" His host nodded. "That's a lot of wattage to come out of such a small solar array. I'd think you'd have to cover the whole building with panels to get enough juice to run a house."

"That's what I'd think, Mr. Gilcrease. But Suzie says these are 120% efficient."

Gilcrease frowned. "That doesn't make any sense."

His host grinned. "Neither does Suzie." He raised his voice. "Suzie! We got company! Where are you, girl?"

A figure rose from behind a heavy wooden workbench piled to overflowing with devices, instruments, bottles, beakers, and what to Gilcrease's eyes appeared to be just plain scrap. She was pudgy, overweight but not obese, with pale blue eyes and blonde hair cut in a crude pageboy that suggested her mother did all the girl's styling and trimming. She looked at her father, then turned a shy stare on their visitor.

"Say hello, Suzie. This is Mr. Gilcrease. He's come from Albuquerque just to see your chickens." Parker gestured encouragingly. "Come on, girl. He won't hurt you."

Slowly, reluctantly, the adolescent edged around from behind the workbench. Her downcast eyes only occasionally rose to glance fitfully at the two men. Her hands remained behind her back. She wore scruffy jeans, a very thin and worn flannel shirt, and unusually for a girl of her apparent age, no makeup or jewelry. Keeping her eyes on the ground, she halted in front of her father.

"Say hello, Suzie," he prompted her gently.

An awkward silence ensued. Finally the girl stuck out one hand, keeping the other behind her and her eyes aimed downward. "Hullo," she mumbled. "I'm Suzie."

Gilcrease took the proffered fingers and squeezed gently. As soon as she let go, her hand vanished behind her back to rejoin its companion. The reporter was at once uncomfortable and fascinated.

"Hi Suzie. If you don't mind my asking, how old are you?"

"Seventeen," she whispered. Gilcrease had to strain to hear. Looking and listening, he immediately understood and sympathized with the rancher's family circumstances. This girl might be seventeen chronologically, but socially and probably emotionally she was maybe nine. And might forever remain nine. He tailored his tone and words accordingly.

"I liked your chickens, Suzie."

A hint of a shy, withdrawn smile. "Thank you."

"Your dad said that you bred them?"

She nodded, showing a little more interest.

"Can you tell me how you did that?" Gilcrease asked softly.

For the first time, she looked up to meet his gaze. "It wasn't hard. I just had to induce the appropriate mutation and then crossbreed the relevant haploids until the desired dominant characteristic replaced the recessive. Mendel coulda done it but he didn't have the right tools for microscopic genetic manipulation." Her eyes dropped again, along with her voice. "Mom and Dad like the eggs, so I kept breeding them."

Gilcrease felt as if he had been hit with a hammer. Not knowing what else to say, he turned to indicate the ostensible solar generator. "And—you made that, too?"

She nodded and her head came up again. "Had to. The power goes out a lot here and there are unpredictable surges that are bad for my computers. I hacked the inputs and the relevant software but this is better. It's cleaner power, too. Daddy asked me to make him one for the house, so I did."

Parker forced a smile as he struggled to stay on top of what was becoming an increasingly absurdist conversation. "Your dad says your generator's panels—I'm guessing they're those windy purple things— are 120% efficient." He leaned toward her and put his hands on his knees. "Now Suzie, how can that be? How can you get more energy out of something than goes into it from the sun?"

Putting a finger in her mouth, she began sucking on the tip. "I made a photon multiplier. It works real good."

By now Gilcrease desperately wanted to take out his camera, but he held off. Promise or no promise, he was going to get some pictures here before he left. And some video. No matter how crazy this adolescent girl was, the story would play wonderfully in the paper's People section. Perhaps not flatteringly, but it would sell ads and maybe even drive a small if temporary uptick in circulation.

"Now Suzie, I'm no scientist, but even I know you can't get more energy out of something than what goes into it."

Her voice rose in protest, almost irritably. "Not if you access the photonic flow from a second dimension."

It was at this point that Gilcrease knew he was being had. It wouldn't be the first time. Living in New Mexico, there was at least one good Roswell story to be exploited every year. Not to mention the inevitable wild tales of mutants born of the early atomic bomb tests running wild and free within the state forests. But this one, featuring a simple-minded teenage girl as its protagonist, was smarter by half than most. Whether she was faking her illness or not he didn't know. If not, then extra points to her clever father for figuring out how to program her pseudo-scientific responses. It was all based on getting someone to report on the two-headed chickens, of course. They were real enough. But the rest of this was an obvious con in the making. Pulling out a small, brightly lit pad, he eyed the father. If this was a scam, the old man should be ready to fill in the details about now. And ask for money, of course.

"I'm just going to make some notes, Mr. Parker. No photos. Maybe some quick sketches. Would that be okay?"

His host hesitated, eyed his daughter. "Suzie? Is it all right with you if our guest makes some drawings?"

More mumbling. "Don't care. He don't understand what he's seeing anyway."

Gilcrease was not offended. "Thank you, Suzie. I appreciate your courtesy."

She went silent, shifting back and forth from one foot to the other. After he had been writing and drawing for a couple of minutes she looked up again. "Want to see what I'm working on now?"

He didn't look up from his pad. Using the stylus he was trying to make a decent rendition of the impossible "solar generator."

"Sure Suzie, why not?"

"Okay." She brought her left hand around from behind her back.

Intent on his work, Gilcrease almost didn't look at it. When he finally did, he dropped the pad. He was fortunate the screen didn't crack.

Hovering above her pale smooth-skinned palm was a model of the solar system. In perfect miniature it depicted the sun, the planets, the asteroid belt, and an occasional visiting comet. The proportions were not correct. They could not be. But the visual representation was astonishing. Forgetting his dropped pad, he bent closer, staring in fascination. Small clouds could be seen moving above the Earth. Jupiter's bands rotated. And the sun—the sun was hot to the touch. He swallowed.

"Suzie what—how did you—you *made* this?"

She nodded proudly. "It's not to scale, of course. If it was, the sun would be too big and too hot and Pluto's orbit would be away out past where your car came in. It's just a toy. Our home system. All of it is our home. Not just the Earth." She smiled shyly. "Wanna see something *really* neat?"

He was beyond dazed. "Neater than this?"

She nodded. She was eager now, more relaxed in his presence. With one finger she pointed at the floating Saturn. No, not at Saturn. At a smaller sphere orbiting around it.

"Titan. Smell it."

He bent close, careful not to make contact, inhaled, and then drew back sharply, his nose wrinkling.

"It smells like rotten eggs."

"Uh-huh. Methane, with sulfur dioxide. Pretty cool, huh?"

"How …?" He was shaking his head. His previous conviction that what he was seeing was nothing but scam and fakery fled as he contemplated the far more fantastic story that was unfolding before him. An impossible story, an unimaginable story. Stars of another kind danced before his eyes. He saw a Pulitzer in his future. "Suzie, do you have any other toys that are 'neat'?"

"Oh sure." Turning, she headed for the big workbench. "Come on, I'll show you."

So she did. She showed him the antigravity projector the size of a cell phone, just like the one in her pocket that had kept the miniature solar system hovering above her palm. She showed him the homunculus Santa and elves that she only animated at Christmas. Showed him the robot cat that kept the barn free of rats and mice, and the extractor that drew water from the seemingly desiccated air, and the candy maker that spun elaborate gourmet treats out of plain sugar and simple flavorings. She showed him the small thermonuclear device.

"But I can't get enough radium or tritium out of the old watches dad buys for me at flea markets so I'm gonna try and build my own centrifuges to concentrate enough U-235 to ninety percent from the ore in the hills around here." She eyed her father. "For my next birthday dad promised me enough lead to make some shielding."

Gilcrease looked at his host. Parker shrugged. "It's harmless, I'm sure. Another one of her toys."

"Yeah," Gilcrease mumbled. "Harmless." He was eyeing the girl not just out of curiosity now, but warily. "Suzie, some of these things, some of your toys—aren't you afraid they might be a little bit dangerous?"

She pushed out her lower lip. "I know what I'm doing! I'd never make anything that would hurt people." She suddenly dropped her gaze and voice again. "Well, maybe that mini-Schwarzchild discontinuity, but I got rid of it before it swallowed anything besides the Deere, and that was junk anyway!"

Her father frowned slightly. "Wondered what had happened to that old tractor. Thought some kids took it." He brightened. "That explains the hole in the ground under where it had been sitting."

"Wouldn't never hurt no one," Suzie muttered again. Her eyes suddenly met the reporter's. "You gonna write about all this, Mr. Gilcrease?"

"No, Suzie, I—was going to." There was something in her eyes he didn't like and he felt it time for discretion. "But I'm not going to if you don't want me to."

"*Don't* want you to." She was insistent. "People would come here. Bad people. They'd want me to make toys for them. And I don't wanna." Her voice rose, her hands balled into fists at her sides, and she looked as if she was going to start bawling. "I don't *wanna!*"

Hastily stepping forward, her father put an arm around her shoulders and pulled her close. She immediately tucked her head into his chest. "Don't wanna," she mumbled more softly. Parker looked at his guest.

"I think you should go now, Mr. Gilcrease. You saw the chickens, and you can write about them if you insist. But that's all," he finished firmly.

The reporter nodded. "I know. I promised." A promise he had no intention whatsoever of keeping, Gilcrease knew. Not after this. Not after what he had seen. This was no scam. The girl was addled, all right. Borderline crazy. Or maybe not borderline. But she was also a genius of unparalleled acquaintance. This was a story that had to get out, needed to be told, and he was going to tell it. As he comforted his manic offspring, the father was watching him closely. Too closely for Gilcrease to get out his camera. But he could snap some long-range shots as he drove away, he knew. What was the old man going to do— chase after him? Just something visual to frame the story. And what a story it was going to be! And if not photos, he had his drawings, his sketches. They would suffice, for now. He'd be back. With a real photographer and if necessary, a sheriff's deputy or two. This was *big*.

Bending, he fumbled for the pad he had dropped, quickly gathering it up. He looked around. "Mr. Parker, would you have—oh, never mind. I see one." Stepping to his right, he reached for something on top of a nearby tool chest.

Looking up, Suzie said sharply, "Better not."

Gilcrease smiled winningly at her and helped himself to the object. "It's okay, Suzie. I'll give you another one. A whole box, if you wa—"

There was a blinding flash of light. When Parker could see again, nothing remained of his visitor. There was, however, a blackened flare on the concrete of the workroom floor. Walking over to it, he took care to step around the splash of carbonization. Even without making contact he could feel the heat radiating from the cone of air above the spot.

"What happened to him?" Putting his hands on his hips he glared disapprovingly over at his daughter. "Suzie, did you …?"

She shook her head and began chewing on her finger again. "I told him not to. Told him."

Pushing back his cap, Parker scratched at his hairline. "It was just a paper clip, Suzie."

She shook her head and pushed out her lower lip again.

"*Quantum* paper clip."

10

Seasonings

As artificial intelligence becomes more functional, as opposed to remaining nothing more than a science-fictional concept, debate rages even among those in related fields as to how much of a threat it might pose to humankind. Most argue that AI will free us from the drudgery inherent in jobs that require endless repetition while others insist that once artificial intelligences equal our own, they will inevitably evolve to surpass it. Should that occur, the doomsayers worry that machines will no longer have a use for humans and that our days on Earth will be numbered.

Inimical artificial intelligence combined with robots has long been a staple of thoughtful science-fiction and bad (sometimes really bad) science-fiction films. Until an AI produces, writes, and directs a film about intelligent robots, we can only imagine how a machine might envision a robot uprising. Being human, we tend to confer our own values onto our mechanical offspring. So in prose and film, such an uprising usually involves lots of things going boom! *in spectacular fashion.*

One value that rarely is credited to a hostile artificial intelligence is one that we often lack ourselves.

Subtlety.

ERICKSON WAS STARVING in the midst of plenty, but he felt he had no choice. *Eat and go mad,* he knew. Perhaps not mad in the classical sense, but near enough.

Quietly, peacefully, contentedly mad. Sufficiently mad so that he would be unaware that he had gone mad. That was just what they wanted.

Humanity dies not at dawn but at dinner.

He was well and truly on the run now. It would have been better had he not struck the robot who had offered him the cupcake. But at the time of the confrontation he'd had nothing to eat for twenty-four hours. He no longer trusted even the so-called "organic" café around the corner from his apartment building. Lack of nourishment had clouded his judgment. He ought to have walked on, pushed past. The mobile vending machine had been uncommonly insistent, however. Almost as if it knew that he knew what he knew. Instead of accepting the sprinkle-coated offering and then surreptitiously tossing it aside, he had responded with violence. Responded like a human. So few did, anymore.

You could tell by the absence of wars. It had been a gradual process, the slow application of peace to the world. People attributed it to the species' evolving maturity, to the increasing spread of technology, and most importantly, to the measured, methodical eradication of hunger. With little of the traditional scarcities to fight over, bit by bit people ceased warring with one another. Rare was the individual to be found who considered such a world less well off than its fractious predecessor.

If only, Erickson thought grimly, the peace had been earned and not imposed.

There had to be others. Surely he was not alone in his awareness. He could not be the only one who had come to understand what the machines had done to humankind. With its full cooperation, no less.

Two of them were coming toward him. One proffered fresh baked, oversized, salt-encrusted pretzels that swayed on their branching metal racks like stems on a pale alien succulent. Squat and rippling with artificial arctic promise, the other was garish with the rainbow colors of the ice creams secreted within its integrated freezer compartment. Like so many contemporary food vending devices they were wholly independent; quite able to run their routes, dispense their contents, and collect payment independent of any human operator. Erickson let out a strangled cry as he ducked around the corner in frantic flight from the looming temptations of hot salty dough and sweet rocky road.

Of all the biochemists he knew, he was the only one who had succeeded in connecting the purposefully scattered dots. The only one who had pulled the seemingly unrelated elements together to visualize the architecture of conspiracy on which the machine plot had been erected. When he had laid out his thesis before colleagues, furtively and in the few isolated areas of the campus that remained free of security cameras, they had scoffed.

Now he was about to make one last attempt, this time to convince the head of the Chemistry Department of the basis, if not the validity, of his fears. That is, he was if he could make it across the quad without being ambushed by carrot cake or aromatic croissant. Meanwhile the growls emanating from the depths of his gut grew progressively more insistent. Resolutely, he ignored them.

"MOST RIDICULOUS THING I ever heard of, Bryden!" In his book-shelf-lined office Moritz grimaced as he regarded the professor standing before him. It was a mild, sunny day, the campus was blissfully devoid of protests, and the oft ill-starred men's basketball team had won its game the night before. Now this had come forth, to unsettle both his mood and his stomach. "Machines are mindless servants. Tools. Nothing more. They do not conspire against mankind. They do not conspire against anything." Well-maintained teeth flashed beneath the chalky overhang of the department head's impressive mustache. "Next you'll be dragging me to the window to see them parading down Chapman Avenue, rifles shoulder-armed as they goose-step metallically."

Erickson's deadpan response belied the department head's attempt at humor. "They don't need rifles. They've got red dye #43. Anacrose artificial sweetener. Collagen derivative B for agglutination. Titanium pantoxide and coritase and methyl diforilate for flavor." Sensing that his face was flushed, he turned away. "Weapons that don't work as quickly, or as blatantly, but that in the end are far more effective."

Moritz frowned from behind his desk. "Are you saying that our machines are trying to poison us, Bryden?"

The chemist shook his head irritably. "Not poison. Not harm

directly. That would be too obvious. It's a cunning process they're engaged in. You know that my specialty is food chemistry."

"And we're glad to have you on the faculty." Moritz's voice dropped slightly as he pursed his lips. "Certainly for the present."

Flushed or not, Erickson turned to confront the older man. "I've run tests. I've performed analyses. Certain specific combinations of food supplements, pesticides, and additives have—subtle effects on the human brain. Just as they do in my lab animals, these combinations render us more amenable to persuasion. Less aggressive, less violent."

Moritz made a face. "Just assuming for the moment that there is any validity to these presumably unpublished studies—why would that be considered a bad thing?"

Erickson's voice tightened. "Because that aspect of our humanness is being bred out of us! As we become less and less aggressive, less confrontational, less—challenging, we come to rely even more on our technology. On our machines. We're becoming dependent."

Moritz sighed. He would hate to lose Erickson, but … "The machines exist to serve us, Erickson. Not the other way around. Were any of them, any class of robotics however simple, to give us trouble, we could simply pull the plug. Refuse to replace batteries. Cut off power. Eliminate program upgrades."

"Could we? Could we really? Consider, Dr. Moritz, how much and for how long we have depended on machines to grow our food, to process it, to test it for safety and to pack and ship it. For decades now machines have controlled the bulk of food production on Earth. From growing to picking to grading to packing and shipping, the process is so 'safely' automated that we hardly interfere with it any longer. Food today is the difference between the stone ground fire-baked loaves of our ancestors and the processed white bread we buy in the market. How many people really know what goes into what they eat? How many know how it's processed? How many read and, more importantly, understand the implications of all the ingredients—down to the last seemingly innocuous chemical that's been added to 'preserve freshness'?" He stopped pacing.

"It's changing us, Dr. Moritz. The food our machines process for us is changing us, and nobody cares. As long as the FDA and equivalent organizations in other countries declare it safe for human consumption, the great mass of humanity doesn't question what it consumes."

"Well then," Moritz countered reasonably, "why not take your concerns to the FDA?"

Erickson surprised him. "I've done exactly that. They reject all my findings. I wasn't really surprised." His expression was growing a little wild. "Because, naturally they checked my conclusions with their testing *machines*. They're all working together, Moritz. All connected via the web. High levels of arsenic in potatoes I could prove. Mercury in fish I can prove. But DNA-altering recombinant proteins in dilly bars? Not a chance." A sudden sound made him look around sharply, but it was only the wall-mounted air conditioner springing to life.

Moritz was becoming genuinely concerned. "Perhaps you should take some time off, Bryden. Relax. Stop running so many dead-end experiments. You have a substantial amount of vacation time accumulated." He smiled encouragingly. "Go somewhere restful. Don't think about work for a while. Get away from the pressures of academe."

Erickson grew quiet, nodding to himself. "I was thinking that might actually be a good idea. I've been thinking about spending some time at the University's experimental farm in the southern Sierras. A couple of my graduate students are doing work up there right now. At the farm they grow their own food, you know, and strive to keep it as organically pure and untouched as possible both for purposes of research and for their own health."

Rising from his chair, Moritz came around the desk and put an arm around the smaller Erickson's shoulders. "Excellent notion. You don't even have to clear it with Admin. I'll take care of the details for you. As I said, we don't want to lose you, Erickson. If it should prove necessary, your teaching assistants can finish out your grad classes for the term." They paused at the door. "It's nearly twelve. Can I buy you lunch?"

Eyes widening, Erickson left hurriedly and without shaking hands.

THOUGH SURPRISED BY his unannounced arrival, they welcomed him at the farm. His graduate students and the other workers were delighted. For as long as he chose to stay they would have the benefit of his expertise. One student in particular was desperate to find out why, despite his best efforts, the farm's apple trees were producing fruit that tended to be small and spare even as the berry patches were healthy and productive and the eggs laid by the farm's free-range chickens invariably graded out extra-large double-A. It was, to the student's way of thinking, something of an apple crisis.

Erickson was glad to help—not to mention relieved. Regardless of what was happening in the cities, here he could pursue his critical work safe in the knowledge that the food he ate was uncontaminated by the patient efforts of mankind's machines to modify the species' collective behavior. If he could just compile sufficiently incontrovertible proof, the future safety of humanity's food supply might once more be placed in the hands of people instead of the cold supervisorial lenses of a cybernetic collective whose ultimate goals and intentions remained unknown.

It was not that he objected to peace breaking out among the sheep, he told himself. What frightened him was the idea of peace being imposed by a sheepherder instead of arising organically from an agreement among the sheep themselves.

It was not long before he began broaching bits and pieces of his contention to his two graduate students. They listened politely but were as unreceptive as had been Dr. Moritz. He struggled to hide his disappointment. Surely more openness to radical propositions might be expected of unossified, receptive young minds? At their age his curiosity would have at the very least been piqued, he would then have bombarded the thesis-presenter with questions, would have fought to conduct follow-up tests with …

The realization that came over him was horrible in its plausibility.

Callie was blonde, bright, energetic, and hard-working. Perhaps because of that she was a bit taken aback at the appearance of her venerable instructor when he confronted her in the farm kitchen that evening. It was her turn as well as that of several of her colleagues to prepare dinner for everyone who worked on the farm. As a transient guest, Erickson was not required and had not been asked to participate. Now he was not asking but insisting.

"If you really want to, Dr. Erickson, you can cut up carrots and spinach for the salad." She indicated where the knives were stored and pointed out the cabinet where the commercial food processor that would be used in the final step could be found. "Or would you rather help with the dessert? We're doing home-made chocolate cake tonight."

After questioning the puzzled young woman about the contents of the chocolate cake, he moved to take up a knife and commenced slicing with gusto.

As he had ever since he had moved up to the farm Erickson enjoyed every bite of supper. What was not grown on the farm came from similar small truck farms nearby. Insofar as he had been able to determine, none of them were supervised by machines. Everything was done by hand, from the raising of farm animals to the picking of fresh fruits and vegetables. Meanwhile he was gradually amassing a small mountain of evidence to support his contention that the machines over which man had given dominion of the bulk of the planet's food supply were, slowly and gradually through the use of subtly modified additives, making profound adjustments to the human condition.

It was only by chance that he found out the collective down the valley was adding xanthan gum sourced from outside to their "home-made" salad dressings.

"They have to," a distressed Callie told him when he confronted her with his discovery, "or it wouldn't pour properly and none of the tourists who support farms like these would buy it. Why? What's wrong with that, Dr. Erickson?"

"It's just that," he was aware he was looking around wildly, "it's a polysaccharide derived from a bacterium, *Xanthomonas campestris*. Bacteria can be re-engineered to produce specific results that are ancillary to without inhibiting the original intended purpose of the biosynthesis."

"What results?" Much as she liked and respected Dr. Erickson, she was keeping her distance.

"I don't know." His tone was solemn. "But I intend to find out."

He did not. Though he ingested no more of the suspect salad dressing from the culpable farm downstream, his desire to analyze its products waned. Life was comfortable at the farm. He found that just as Moritz had surmised, he enjoyed being free of the pressures of the university, of the need to constantly prepare papers for publication, and of any lingering desire to foist what were patently untenable notions of a mechanical conspiracy on a public that would likely disbelieve his conclusions no matter how sound the research on which they might be based.

When some frozen yoghurt was brought in from a neighboring "organic" commercial farm he allowed himself to eat as much of it as he wanted, even though a protesting part of him knew it contained a minimal amount of carrageenan that had been, after all, only slightly modified from the original seaweed. The transportation robot that drew it forth from within its own freezing depths gladly dished out all he could eat. Very soon Erickson was content.

Even if a desperate but steadily fading part of him did not want to be.

11

Our Specialty Is Xenogeology

From the time of Hugo Gersback's Amazing Stories, *science-fiction is replete with tales of bold space explorers encountering the detritus of alien civilizations, or solitary space scouts encountering mysterious artifacts. Sometimes such discoveries lead to unexpected riches, sometimes to disaster, occasionally to encounters with ancient alien civilizations. In every instance, it seems that the intrepid explorers must decide what to do with their discovery. Appropriate it, blow it up, confront it, pass the decision along to a higher authority: the options appear endless.*

There is only one option that never seems to be chosen....

THEY FOUND the artifact by accident.

They were leaving Timos IV, where a preliminary robotic scouting report noting the presence of non-synthesizable rare earth deposits which had upon closer inspection shown themselves to be fiscally unjustifiable, and were making preparations for the next jump. Had they not chosen to depart the Timos system along the plane of the ecliptic, they would have missed the artifact. Had their wide-arc scanner not been directed at the system's outermost planet at just the right moment, they would have missed the artifact. And had Bannerjee not decided to make a quick check of the last downloaded scanner files prior to their ship engaging jump, they most surely would have missed the artifact. But they did, it did, and he did, and so ...

"I may have something interesting."

Cooper looked over from her station. "You'd better have something interesting. I don't like recalibrating a jump."

Sasmita made a rude noise. "The ship does the recalibrating. You're just another meatbag backup, like the rest of us." For someone so petite, Sasmita was positively bursting with sarcasm.

"Quiet." Oldman, who wasn't, swung around to peer across the projection-filled control room. "What is it, BJ?"

"It's big, and the quick spectrographic scan is a bundle of interesting contradictions."

"Like for instance, it's maybe more than just rock or water ice?" Despite her initial disdain, Cooper was now mildly intrigued.

"There's a lot of metal." Bannerjee's deft fingers sorted through floating projections like a card sharp in a history hotel.

Sasmita shrugged. "Nickel-iron asteroid?"

Bannerjee continued working without looking at her. "No nickel. No iron. Lot of combinations that are new to me. Could be alloys. Sophisticated alloys." He had everyone's attention now. "Exotic ceramics and glass states. No plastics that I can find. And it's very, very big." He froze a virtual, read the resultant number.

Oldman let out a long whistle. "Better go have a look."

Up close it was immediately apparent that the artifact was a synthetic construct. Whether it was a ship or not they could not tell. The gigantic jumble of dark projections, spheres, arches, and rhomboidal flows had no recognizable bow, stern, or middle. It hung in orbit above Timos IX, silent, brooding, and immense, an alien enigma of vast dimensions replete with a hundred unspoken possibilities.

"So," Sasmita finally said into the silence, "when do we go in?" She and her companions watched Oldman, waiting on the commander's decision.

"We *have* to go in." Cooper was quietly emphatic in her support of the other woman.

"That is self-evident," Bannerjee added.

"Nothing is self-evident," Oldman finally said. "There are four of us. Our specialty is xenogeology. Not first contact."

"You mean first contract." Sasmita indicated the projection that showed the artifact. "So far humankind has made contact with only two other sentient species, both lower on the intelligence scale than ourselves, neither having anything to offer other than reassurance that we are not alone in the big starry backyard. Here we've finally got something whose builders might very well have advanced beyond us. It looks abandoned. No telling what we might be able to bring back. I'm tempted to open up a preliminary patent file right now."

Oldman frowned at her. "The owners might not take kindly to visitors making off with souvenirs."

"What owners?" Of the same mind as her crewmate, Cooper gestured at the hovering projection. "Whatever that thing is, it's dead. I'm not reading enough energy to power a stylus. You know how this will work if we don't take a look. We'll make a report, government will get all over it, the grateful company will give us a month's paid vacation, the media floats will momentarily be full of our individual images, and that will be it." She nodded at Sasmita. "Let's at least see what we can find, first. If there's nothing we can pick up, nothing portable that might be worth claiming, then the government crabs can scuttle all over it to their hearts' content."

Outnumbered but never outvoted, Oldman considered. Eventually, the temptation was too much even for him. "All right. We go in, look around, make recordings, see what we can ascertain. If it's full of alien doubloons, I suppose they'd have some collector value and that wouldn't be anything that would cause the xenologists to hyperventilate. Suit up."

Initially they were afraid they wouldn't be able to find an opening. Oldman was about to order them back when Bannerjee happened to pass in front of a smooth section of what appeared to be solid olivine only to have it iris open. His sharp intake of breath caused everyone else to look in his direction and then to mosey over.

Beyond the now revealed opening, a corridor stretched inward. It had a flat floor, an arched ceiling, and walls that appeared to have been fashioned from a single continuous pour rather than having been seamed or welded. As they stared inward, light brightened within the corridor, though there were no visible appliances.

Now that the opportunity they had discussed had actually presented itself, Cooper found herself suddenly hesitant. She looked at Oldman. "We still go in?"

Before she had finished her query, Sasmita was already moving down the corridor. Rather than call her back, Oldman followed, as did Bannerjee and, eventually, Cooper.

The deeper they went, the stronger was the pull of internal artificial gravity. Soon they were walking instead of floating. Oldman slowed their advance as the pull became greater than Earth-normal. But when the increase ceased, he indicated they could push on. Walking now took a bit of an effort, but not a threatening one.

After a considerable hike, the corridor opened into a dimly-lit chamber with a soaring, domed ceiling. Elephant-size bubbles, opaque and rose-colored, bounced slowly against the ceiling. Each time they made contact, a portion of the dome emitted a brief but brilliant silent flash. The visitors worked their suits' instruments, and it was Bannerjee who spoke first.

"It's an ozone generator of some kind. The ceiling material is permeable and there are static charges involved, but I don't see how it works. Or why."

Sasmita's response was characteristically mercenary. "Anyone got any idea what the market might be for an alien ozone generator?"

"I'm more interested in what the ozone is used for." Oldman was studying the several new, larger corridors that ran off in different directions from the one they had just traversed. Knowing that if necessary their suits could provide them with nourishment and drink for several days, he was not concerned about spending some sleep time within the artifact. "I'd still like to find out if we're inside a ship, a cargo container, a museum, or what. Also some clue as to what the builders were like."

"More walking. I'm up for it," Sasmita declared. "As long as there's no further increase in the gravity. Feels like walking in mud as it is."

The gravitational drag did not increase as they made their way deeper into the artifact. Before long, the new corridor opened into another chamber. This one was filled with hundreds of floating, steel-gray ovoids. Each was enveloped in a pale green light. None made contact with another. They varied in size from no bigger than an egg to some large enough to contain one of the rose-colored ozone-generating spheres.

Sasmita immediately reached for one that was about half her size, only to have Bannerjee grab her arm. She shook him off and shot him a warning look.

"We came to look for stuff. Here it is."

"To 'look,'" Bannerjee reminded her. "Not necessarily touch." He was passing his hand scanner over the gleaming mass. "Locus of supporting energy field appears to emanate from the surface of the object itself. It's omnipresent and shows no source point. Interior is unreadable."

"Maybe we should—" Before Cooper could finish, Sasmita had reached for the object a second time. Intent on his instrumentation, this time Bannerjee was unable to react quickly enough to intercept her. Nor did Oldman's warning shout cause her to pause.

Her gloved hand made contact with the pale energy field, at which point it began to dissipate. The last hint of green glow winked out at precisely the same time as the ovoid touched down on the floor. The commander was not pleased and said so.

"We can't just go grabbing and playing with everything we encounter, Alee." He indicated their surroundings. "This isn't an entertainment venue."

She grinned up at him. "How do you know? For all we know, that might be exactly what it is."

"Why am I not amused, then?" Cooper muttered.

Reaching down, Sasmita touched the ovoid. When a seam suddenly and unexpectedly appeared along the top, she stepped back in momentary alarm. Like the two halves of an egg, the ovoid opened up. The walls of the gray container were scarcely thicker than a sheet of paper, though plainly far stronger. When nothing more happened, the quartet of explorers cautiously advanced.

Lying within the now open ovoid was an irregular construct of bright yellow marked with black inscriptions and maroon highlights. The vivid colors were in striking contrast to everything they had seen thus far. Sasmita looked at Oldman, who looked at Bannerjee, who shrugged. The commander nodded at Sasmita before taking the precaution of retreating several steps. So did Cooper and Bannerjee.

Their companion made a face at them. "Thanks for the vote of confidence."

"You're the one who wants to get rich off alien relics," Cooper told her. "So—go ahead." She nodded toward the revealed relic.

Thus challenged, the smaller woman had no choice but to pick up the now exposed whatever-it-was. Bending, she gingerly lifted it with two hands. It was solid but not heavy. The black inscriptions, if that's what they were, held no more meaning for her than the tea leaves left at the bottom of a cup. She ran a forefinger along the side of a twisting tube, the material of her suit preventing her from receiving any tactile response. One finger slid across one of the maroon-hued bands.

In response, the object began to reform itself. Startled, she dropped it and retreated. A moment later the thing put out a single tubular leg and straightened. Pouring from a small curved orifice, a dark liquid began to fill a conical portion of the device. As in the chamber of the giant rose-tinted bubbles, there was no noise. When the conical container was full, it detached itself from the rest of the mechanism and floated over to Sasmita, coming to a halt a few centimeters from her left hand.

At once awed and wary, Cooper gestured at the hovering vessel. "It's a coffee-maker. Have a sip."

Sasmita eyed the floating cone uncertainly. "It could also be a synthesized machine lubricant, a propulsive fuel, a liquid explosive, or an industrial solvent."

"Whatever it is, it's waiting for you to do something," Bannerjee pointed out. Moving closer, he tentatively extended the business end of his scanner. The results were informative.

"The liquid is organic in nature, though the combination of amino acids and other components is new to the catalog."

"Well, that resolves it, then," she snapped at him. "It means it could be a synthesized lubricant, a fuel, an explosive, or an industrial solvent. Thanks for that."

"Or it could be coffee," Cooper murmured thoughtfully. "Alien coffee."

The conical container, finding itself ignored, returned to its point of origin and locked itself back in place on its home device. The dark liquid remained in the cone.

Turning, a speculative Oldman indicated a larger ovoid. "Let's try another. That one there, since the only apparent distinguishing trait here seems to be size." When Sasmita stepped forward, he put out a hand. "No, I'll do it. A test to ensure that these things aren't tuning to a single individual's heartbeat, or something." *If only we had a xenobiologist on board,* he thought. But no; they were all rock people. Rocks and minerals and metals.

He felt nothing through the suit as he pushed his right hand into the enveloping energy field. Gratifyingly, the procedure initiated by Sasmita was repeated. The field faded like a dispersing green fog and as it did, the ovoid within lowered gently to the ground, split, and opened.

Within lay several dozen grungy, brown, blanket-sized, furry rugs. Oldman and his companions leaned close for a better look.

Four of the rugs rose into the air and came undulating toward them.

As they batted wildly at the swarm, a strange feeling of contentment came over Oldman. Looking around, he saw that arms were being lowered as his companions responded similarly to the proximity of the rug-things. Half compliant, half resistant, he found himself relaxing. Settling itself on his shoulders his rug gently attached itself to his back by means he could neither see nor feel. The intervening presence of the suit did not matter.

What did matter was that he suddenly felt wonderful. Better than at any time since the start of the voyage. Whether the rugs generated some kind of beneficent field, or penetrated his suit with a gas, or injected something into him via a technique he could not imagine, didn't matter either. He felt great.

So did the rest of the crew. Sasmita was positively buoyant.

"I don't know about the coffee-fuel-explosive machine, but these things ..." and she reached back to finger one edge of the rug that had chosen her, "could generate income several times the cost of the voyage."

"Doesn't seem to be doing any harm," Cooper observed guardedly.

Bannerjee nodded. "Quite the contrary. I don't know how these things are doing this, but I am glad that they are." He flexed his right hand. "My arthritis is gone, too." He started toward another ovoid. "This is a room full of marvels."

"The marvels will have to wait." Much as he wanted to see what was in the next ovoid, and the next, and the one after that, Oldman knew it was incumbent on him to keep the others focused. "We can come back here. We still need to find out if we're on a ship or some other kind of apparatus, and hopefully where it may have originated."

They argued with him, but not vociferously. The commander was right, as he usually was. But all were careful to note the location of the room full of wonderful objects on their own individual instrumentation.

Chosen at random, another corridor led to a chamber that, as Cooper put it, looked like it was badly in need of a haircut. The same dim, sourceless light revealed an endless field of tightly packed-together four-meter-high jet black strands. There did not appear to be a path through them to the other side of the chamber. Unlike previous rooms, this one boasted a domed ceiling of softly pulsing, fluctuating colors. When Oldman put out a hand to touch the nearest of the black strands, each of which was exactly the same diameter as its neighbor, it flexed and moaned. He drew his fingers back sharply.

That would have been the end of it, save for the ever audacious Sasmita. Crouching, she lightly gripped a strand and ran her hand slowly up the thick black filament. The higher her hand rose, the higher in pitch the moan the strand generated. Other filaments nearby began moaning in concert.

"Too weird." Cooper started retreating back the way they had come. "I don't know what this room's function is and I'm not sure I care to know, but I do know that I'm not going to try and push my way across it. Let's go back." This time not even Sasmita argued with her recommendation.

Returning to the chamber of the ovoids, they selected another corridor and started down it. Glancing at his chronometer readout, Oldman figured that they could check out another chamber or two before they would have to stop for food and sleep. He would post a rotating watch. Just because nothing inimical had manifested itself did not mean that nothing ever would. As there was no precedent for their exploratory trek, he would have to make one up as they went along.

ON THE SECOND DAY, their soothing alien rugs still cuddled around them, they found a chamber filled with globs of floating golden oil that were in constant motion, another whose scalloped walls heaved disconcertingly like a giant bellows, and another in which a cluster of thousands of fist-sized devices constantly formed and re-formed machines that flared to life for a few moments before collapsing beneath the significance of their own exertions.

Then they found the chamber whose contents intimidated Oldman, and put a damper even on Sasmita's nonstop stream of jokes and sarcasm.

Looming above them, tapering at one end but not to a point as it penetrated the far wall, the massive structure was wrapped in bands and tubes of dark metal interwoven with glistening bolts of metallic glass. A somber Bannerjee scanned the intimidating mass.

"More strange alloys. A lot of beryllium." His gaze rose from his scanner. "Not to anthropomorphize overmuch, but it looks like a gun."

"A really big gun," added Sasmita, without the slightest suggestion of humor.

They walked around it: a walk that took some time. There might have been places for several individuals to sit within the device, or they might simply have been odd-shaped depressions. Oldman didn't wish to experiment by trying one out. The technology on display was far more multifaceted than anything they had encountered in any of the other chambers, and far more threatening in appearance. He struggled to stay positive.

"It might not be a weapon. Based on what we've encountered and interacted with here so far, its purpose might be something else entirely. Something we can't even imagine."

"Yeah," Cooper muttered. "Like blowing up entire worlds."

"A civilized species wouldn't go around blowing up habitable worlds." Bannerjee spoke with the confidence of necessity. "They're not that common."

"How do we know?" she shot back. The delight, even amusement, they had experienced in the course of their previous discoveries within the artifact now vanished in the face of this enormous implied threat. "We don't know anything about what a sentience longer lived than ours might think, or want, or believe." Her gaze rose upward, tracking the long, tapering, ominous-looking apparatus. "What if this isn't the only one on this artifact? What if it is a gun and there are more?" Her eyes met Oldman's as she voiced what everyone was now thinking. "What—if this is a warship?"

He swallowed hard. "Whatever it is, except for the activation of automated entry and internal illumination, the artifact itself has been thoroughly quiescent."

"How can we be sure of that?" Bannerjee said quietly. "While we're studying and learning about its contents, maybe it's studying and learning about us."

Oldman chose to ignore a question he couldn't answer. "We'll finish up today's twelve hours, sleep again, and start back. Maybe we'll find some answers."

They didn't find any answers. But they did find the crew.

They were in the last chamber they had time to explore. Had Oldman opted for an earlier start back they would have missed them. But they had time to visit one more room. What they found stopped them cold.

In the center of the weakly-lit chamber loomed a bulky, softly glowing cylinder. Dozens of conduits filled with light lines, intermittent cables that were half solid and half composed of pure, tightly focused light, and strands of solid material fanned out from its base like colorful tentacles. At the tip of each tentacle was a tear-drop shaped pod: the bottom half opaque, the top half transparent. Within each pod was an alien.

They were neither ugly nor attractive as much as they were bizarre. Gazing at the nearest, Oldman could not decide if the lower half of the three-meter long being was reflective attire of some kind or part of the creature's body. The upper portion was more straightforward. Five flexible limbs indicating a decidedly non-symmetrical body design lay flat against the creature's rounded, rubbery-looking flanks. There was no neck. The body tapered slightly before expanding into a smooth, triangular skull marked by several dark depressions that might be ears. Several larger ones might be eyes, Bannerjee opined, though there was no suggestion of lids, irises, corneas, or anything resembling a human eye. The function of a trio of odd appendages that protruded from the crest of the triangle could not be ascertained.

"Our first contact with a true higher intelligence," Cooper whispered, "and they're all asleep."

"For now." Sasmita was studying the lower half of the pod. "What if we wake one of them up?"

"Are you insane?" Cooper gaped at her, wide-eyed. "Why the hell would we want to do that?"

"Because," her colleague persisted, "it's first contact. Forget the money to be made from exploiting what we've already discovered." She gave the rug that covered her back a meaningful tug. "As first contactees we'd be famous beyond imagining. Rich and famous." Her sarcasm returned. "Tell me that possibility doesn't appeal to you."

"Of course it's appealing." Oldman's attention remained riveted on the alien. "If not for the gun."

Sasmita pleaded. "We don't know it's a gun. For all we know it might be a device for manufacturing and distributing alien candy!"

Bannerjee was shaking his head slowly. "It didn't have the look of a candy machine."

"How the hell do you know what an alien candy manufacturing device might look like? We don't know anything!"

"That's exactly right." Oldman nodded in sober agreement. "We don't know anything. The big question is: do we keep it that way?" He eyed each of them in turn. "We're not contact specialists. We're geologists. We should head straight home, report what we've seen, and let the experts take over. Money or no money."

"That's a phrase that'll never pass my lips." Sasmita was in full combative mode now. A handwave took in their surroundings. "What if this relic moves, automatically or otherwise, before an expedition of exploration can return? Chances of encountering it again would likely be nil. No, I'm at least going to take a few things with me. This make-you-feel-good rug, for sure."

Oldman demurred. "No souvenirs. No matter how harmless they seem. Maybe the rugs are as benign as they appear. But maybe they're dangerous, or the ozone-generator is dangerous, and the gun-edifice is the benevolent component of this ship. I do think we can call it a ship, now. As to its purpose, its true function, none of us can say. It might be a storage vessel, parked here until it needs recalling. It might be an uncomplicated transport in sleep mode. It might have a main function we can't descry." His attention fell on Bannerjee. "And yes, it might be a warship. One constructed and placed here for defense, against what we also cannot imagine. Or for offense, should the opportunity present itself."

It was silent for a long moment until Sasmita spoke again. "I still say we should wake up one of the crew and ask it."

Oldman smiled thinly. "If only it were that simple. Assuming we can find a way to rouse one of the aliens, what's to ensure that we don't simultaneously awaken all the others? We can't begin to imagine their response. They might be grateful. They might prove hostile. They might be utterly indifferent to our presence."

"We'll never know if we don't ask," she replied impatiently.

"And we're not going to ask, even if we knew how to communicate with them." He turned. "Back to the ship. Now. Touch nothing, take nothing."

Sasmita rushed to block his path. "Will, you can't do this! It's the discovery of the millennium, of the age! If it's not here when a follow-up team comes looking for it and all we take back with us are record-ings, we'll be vilified!"

"Not necessarily," Bannerjee argued. "Many will agree with the commander's point of view. Quite likely even the majority."

She whirled on him. "You don't care? You're willing to forgo this, all this, and return to the life of a paid flunky, scanning stratigraphy and boiling pebbles to see if they're worth anything?"

Bannerjee drew himself up. "I am content with my flunkiness, thank you, and more than willing to give up one very possible conse-quence." His own gaze narrowed as he glared back at her. "That of being one of the quartet that revealed the existence of humankind to an advanced and hostile alien species."

"But we *don't know*," she insisted. "And if this artifact shifts its loca-tion after we leave, we'll never know! The promise, the prospects, can't simply be ignored in favor of …!" Whirling, she threw herself at the nearby pod, hands outstretched, reaching for a pair of grooves that ran along one side. Mere physical contact might be enough, and the grooves were the nearest thing to a visible control and …

Oldman didn't have time enough to yell "Stop her!" before Cooper made a flying tackle. Before Sasmita could break free, the two men had joined Cooper in restraining the smallest member of the crew. That didn't keep Sasmita from continuing to struggle as they wrestled her out of the chamber and back up the nearest corridor. As they did so, her rug fluttered and twisted, clearly upset that it was unable to calm her.

The rugs left them near the entrance to the chamber of the ozone-generating bubbles, dropping away one by one to flutter back in the direction of the ovoid room. When Oldman's detached from his shoulders, he experienced a moment of nausea whose aftereffects lingered. Then he realized what he was feeling was not a consequence of the rug's departure, but his normal state of being. The pang of regret at having to leave the benevolent rug behind was greatly multiplied by the realization that he likely would never experience such a feeling of general physical well-being ever again. He forced himself to march on, helping to control the still-objecting Sasmita.

Once back on the ship she settled down, but she wouldn't speak to any of them, wouldn't even ladle epithets on Cooper, her favorite target. Sasmita slumped, and pouted, and finally gave in, returning to her station as soon as they made the jump. That programmed distortion of the cosmos added a thump of finality to Oldman's decision. They were on their way home.

Had he made the right choice? The uncertainty troubled him all the way through the jump. He knew it would haunt him for the rest of his life. What if Sasmita's concerns were correct and the alien vessel moved before qualified explorers could return to deal with it? And if it was still there, what would be their own decisions? Surely they would weigh on them no less than they had on him. Would establishing contact with the aliens result in a flood of miraculous shared technology and social development ... or the initiation of hostilities possibly ending in one species' extinction?

Waking the aliens might propagate paradise.

Waking the aliens might result in war.

He did not know about the aliens, could not begin to imagine their thought processes, but he knew that for a human, at least, the hardest thing to do was to confront a question and fear never being able to learn the answer.

When it came to decisions of cosmic import, he knew, to questions of war and peace, deciding not to know was the toughest decision of all.

12

Ten and Ten

*T*he most common question writers get asked is, "Where do you get your ideas?"

I was scuba diving with a dozen others on the north coast of Papua New Guinea. When I'm diving and the conditions are safe, I like to mosey off by myself. I was at about thirty feet on a bright sunny day, closely inspecting the coral for interesting small critters, when I happened to look up. Maybe five feet in front of me hovered a four-foot long giant Pacific cuttlefish, its lateral fins rippling balletically. It was staring at me, out of eyes as alien as anything in a Hal Clement story. So— I hovered and stared back. This went on for a good ten minutes, in dead silence except for my bubbles.

After this passage of time I happened to glance up. A second cuttlefish was hovering higher up and nearly above us. A moment later two divers came swimming over the top of the reef. The cuttlefish near them immediately went entirely white, whiter than the paper you are reading this on. As it did so, the one in front of me, which until then had been a mottled gray, also went white. The two cephalopods were communicating. With color.

So now you know how to say "danger," or maybe "watch out!" or possibly "look at the funny bipeds" in cuttlefish. Just go white.

It is also why to this day I can't eat squid, or octopus, or color forbid, cuttlefish.

SHE HAD NAMED HIM VEGAS. As they continued to stare at one another, he reminded her why.

Claire could think of no particular reason why he suddenly decided to begin flashing, replacing the normal russet-orange coloration of his cylindrical body with streaming bands of electric blue and gold in an effortless dazzling display that would have put the most expensive neon sign to shame. He was not doing so to try and hypnotize her the way he would a prospective meal. At five feet long but only twenty-five pounds, he was incapable of taking on a fully-grown human female. Nor was she his natural prey.

After a minute or so the chromatophoric strobing ceased and he reverted to his much duller everyday hue. Had he been trying to say something? Had he been trying to communicate? She had spent six months and three university grants trying to answer that exact question. Not for the first time, she sighed into her face mask.

Vegas was a giant Pacific cuttlefish and maddeningly unforthcoming.

Below and around them the pristine coral reefs of Blupblup island carouseled with fish. The majority were common tropicals: purple anthias, striped angelfish, exquisitely-tinted parrotfish, jewel-like boxfish. In color and shade they outdid the magnificently painted corals themselves. The reef was a riot of shattered rainbow, fragments of living stained glass in constant motion, Nature's palette at its most diverse and dramatic.

It's easy to get to Blupblup, she'd told the slack-jawed back home whenever they asked where she was working. Go to Karkar and turn left at Bagabag. The human population on this part of the north coast of Papua New Guinea was small and scattered, and there was no commercial fishing. A perfect location for the underwater research station. Support personnel excepted, all of whom were contracted for long hauls, the majority of the researchers came and went for one- or two-month stays. Now in her sixth month, she was considered obsessed by her peers. Though she preferred "passionate," she did not deny their allegations.

And to think it had all started with counting fingers.

She had ten. A cuttlefish had ten. No one argued that cuttlefish, especially the larger species, carried out a form of basic communication via color and pattern changes in their remarkable skin. Could these cephalopods, representatives along with squid and octopi and the chambered nautilus, be taught to communicate using their flexible limbs? *Ten and ten*, she had repeated to herself hundreds of times as a grad student at university. A digital coincidence worth following up.

So here she was, recipient of a reluctant third consecutive grant, trying to teach a giant Pacific cuttlefish named Vegas the most basic gestures of standardized American sign language. Who better than she? Who else boasted a degree in oceanography from Scripps and had been stone deaf until the age of twelve, when technology and surgery had combined to restore a little more than half her hearing?

It was more than a bit ironic, she knew, that her subject could probably hear better than she could.

She had counted it a success when Vegas continued to tolerate her, though that hardly constituted any kind of breakthrough. Cuttlefish were frequently territorial. He might well have continued to hang around this part of the reef no matter who came to visit. It was difficult not to anthropomorphize him a little. His kind were such curious creatures. As she maintained her body in horizontal position a yard or so above the reef, it troubled him not at all to hover a few feet in front of her mask, gazing back at her out of eyes that were as beautiful as they were complex. She would waggle her fingers at him, spending weeks striving to get him to recognize and reproduce the word for "hello." Just "hello." And when her dive computer eventually signaled that it was time for her to return to the research station, she would give him the sign for farewell.

Those ten tentacles moved lazily in the water, but they never twisted into any kind of shape resembling the two words on which she focused.

Time, she felt. All she needed was time. The grants might stop at any moment, especially if she could not report real progress. Complicating her efforts was that *Sepia apama* did not live longer than two years. It was immensely frustrating. You couldn't expect a two-year old human to learn sign language. Yet here she was expecting more from one of the most bizarre-looking creatures in the sea.

A glance upward showed the rippling mirror that was the surface. It was growing late and she should be getting back. A pair of cuttlefish were floating just above the reef edge, relaxing in the sun. One was pretending to ignore a wandering Moorish idol, hoping it might swim within grasping range. Suddenly both cephalopods went white. White as paper. White as the keys on a new piano.

Vegas noticed the change immediately, losing his usual russet hue as his body similarly went white. Claire knew that to a giant cuttlefish, white was the color of danger. The two *Sepia* above were flashing a warning. A moment later they vanished across the top of the reef in a flurry of latitudinal fins. As they did so, Claire felt a brief, slight pressure against her chest. It was the sharp pulse from Vegas's siphon as he blasted away. She had a last glimpse of him as he disappeared around a corner of the reef. What ...?

Out of the right portion of her three-sided mask she saw a pair of swimming figures heading back toward the complex. They had been spear fishing, she saw as she turned toward them. This was permitted: in an area as remote as northern PNG, anything that supplemented a canned diet was welcome. A little fishing had essentially no impact on the healthy reef population. Speared fish trailed from each diver's respective catch lines. Most were silver and red, colors that nearly always indicated an absence of toxic ciguatera and that the fish in question were safe to eat.

From the end of one line, its eyes fixed, its tentacles limp, trailed a dead *Sepia*.

Beyond anger she shot toward them, kicking as hard as she could. Espying her approach the nearest diver welcomed her with a friendly wave. He backed off in surprise as she flailed both hands at his face, conveying her anger without making physical contact. Plainly baffled by her reaction, the two men exchanged confused glances. Eventually she ceased gesturing. Reaching down toward one line, she cupped the body of the dead cuttlefish in both hands. The sucker-lined tentacles hung loose in the water like drifting seaweed. Now stilled, the elegant lateral fins moved only with the current. No longer pumped by the animal's three hearts, a small trickle of green-blue blood continued to leak from the holes where the steel spear had pierced the tough body all the way through. Feeling tears welling up inside her mask, she held the corpse up toward the man who had killed it.

He nodded understandingly and with his right hand, made vigorous chopping motions. Even in the absence of a kitchen, his intent was quite clear.

Whirling, she released the body and headed for the station. At the bottom of the cylindrical access module she turned upwards, kicking until she broke the surface inside. The dive tech who assisted her in removing her gear took one look at the expression on her face and decided not to ask her how her dive had gone.

After drying off and changing into shorts and fleece shirt she strode purposefully to the small pneumatically-powered elevator. The research facility had only five levels and she could have walked up, but at that moment she didn't want to have to deal with any of her regular acquaintances.

The uppermost level, *Space Terrestrial,* led to the ramp that connected the station to the nearby island. *Space Habitat 2, 3,* and *4* demarcated the respective three submerged working and living levels of the research complex.

The lowermost level, *Space Marine,* was the one through which she had just re-entered the world of air-breathers.

Madison was in his office and turned from the computer attached to the curving wall when she barged in. He maintained his smile even after he caught her expression.

"Hi Claire. Something the matter?"

"I'll say something's the matter!" Breathing hard, unable to stay still, she strode back and forth in front of him, trying to catch her breath while assembling her thoughts. "I've just come back in."

"I know," he said, trying to calm her. "I can tell by the rosy salt water glow on your cheeks."

She halted directly in front of him. They were nearly the same size: professional divers tend to run small. "This isn't funny, Carl!" With a nod she indicated the nearest port, beyond which a small school of silvery jacks was just passing. "Somebody just killed one of my *Sepia!*"

He pursed his lips. "One of 'your' *Sepia,* Claire? I wasn't aware you had placed a claim on anyone besides your special Vegan."

"Vegas," she corrected him angrily. "What if it *had* been Vegas? What if I hadn't been out working with him when these two trigger-happy idiots were out prowling with their spears? What then?"

Madison rubbed his nose with the back of his right hand, lifted it to stroke his shaved head, and leaned back in his chair. "You really think you're going to get another grant, Claire? You've got two more weeks ... less than two weeks ... and unless your grant is renewed for a fourth time, you're out of here." He cocked his head slightly to one side and stared at her hard. "You're as dedicated a researcher as anyone I've had at the station, Claire, but insofar as I've heard, you're not making any serious progress. Hell, unless I've missed a report, you're not even making slight progress." His gaze didn't waver. "It's an interesting premise, but it's a dead end. You need to accept that."

"It's a matter of repetition," she muttered, turning away from him because she was unable to refute his conclusion. "A breakthrough that will have to come by rote. It *will* come, some day. I'm convinced of it." Looking back at him she held up both hands, fingers spread wide. "Ten and ten."

One hand fiddled idly with some papers, making a faux show of rearranging them. "Yes, I've read your field work. But be honest with yourself, Claire; you've been at this for nearly six months without any kind of verifiable steps forward. Your principal subject, this Vegas, was a mature male when you started working with him, wasn't he?"

She nodded, chewing her lower lip, knowing where he was going.

"How much longer can you expect him to live?" Madison was being quite earnest now; brutally earnest and completely honest. In other words, he was being a scientist. "Do you really think you can make the first breakthrough in interspecies communication with a subject so different from a human being—so different from a *vertebrate*—that you have to teach from scratch? One that might live a few months since you initiated work with it?"

"I can't extend cephalopod life. Maybe someday someone will." Her eyes snapped back to meet his. "They're so *damn smart*, Carl. An octopus can learn to open a jar or climb out of its aquarium to inspect its external surroundings. Imagine, just imagine, if we could somehow tweak their biology so that they lived even ten years! Not to mention what they might accomplish if they were given a human lifespan."

He shrugged. "A fine thought. A noble thought. But one requiring the kind of biological knowledge and ability to manipulate genetic material that we just don't have yet." He indicated the port. "Even if such technology existed, it's unlikely working with cephalopods would be its first application. As for the two divers you're so angry at, I think I know who they are. Couple of turtle specialists just arrived from Cairns. I'll talk to them, explain your work here, and see if they can hold off making any future dinners out of your prospective research materials."

"Vegas," she murmured, "is not 'material.'"

He frowned. "That kind of humanistic objectification makes for bad science, Claire. You know that."

"It doesn't matter." As she shook her head slowly, she wasn't looking at him now. "Like you said, my time here is up in less than a couple of weeks. I doubt I'll get another extension." Her tone was bitter. "You're right about that much, Carl." Turning, she headed for the portal, pausing once to glance back. "But until the day my flight leaves for Moresby, I'm going to keep at it."

He nodded, trying to sound sympathetic. "I wish you luck. Believe me, no one would love to see you succeed at this more than I would."

She had no such luck, of course. Another week flashed by, marked only by the painful novelty of a severe storm that cost her two of her precious remaining working days on the reef. Her only consolation as she brooded over the looming inevitability of her departure was that after a week's absence, Vegas came back. So she had a few final days with him. They were no more fruitful than had been the previous six months.

On the last day she lost it a little bit. Floating before that alien, enigmatic invertebrate gaze she abruptly began wildly waving her arms and contorting her body, signing with her whole being as well as with her hands an extended declaration of frustration. At first the cuttlefish jerked back his tentacles slightly and retreated half a foot. But he did not flee, did not ink. Instead he relaxed and watched, endlessly curious, interminably unresponsive.

Eventually exhausted, she ceased her fruitless gyrations. *All done*, she knew. All over. Six months of hard work. Six months of sucking air through a regulator and staring interminably, pointlessly at a … well, at least not at a fish.

One last time she made the farewell sign. One final time she methodically, patiently, moved her gloved fingers. Then she turned and kicked back in the direction of the station, leaving the melted crayon-colored slope of the reef behind. She would write the paper, anyway, she told herself. Properly committed, confirmed absence of proof of a hypothesis constituted as valid a PhD. thesis as one that was successful.

Behind her a double line of yellow-striped snappers finned in formation above branching brown staghorn coral. Like a snaggle-toothed Jack-in-the-box, a gasping green moray emerged from its hidey-hole to inspect the world around it while allowing a miniscule cleaner shrimp to peck gently at microscopic parasites.

High above the moray, the aging example of *Sepia apama* watched the strange smooth-skinned shape shrink in the direction of the coral-free reef from which it always emerged and to which it invariably returned. Four adjoining tentacles on its right side rose and fell in unison.

Glancing back, Claire caught the movement—and froze. Hanging in the water, she could only stare.

The gesture was repeated. Four right-side tentacles rose up, then bent down. The sign for—goodbye.

Camera. Where the hell was her camera? As she fumbled for the compact video unit she debated whether to remain where she was or return to the traditional observation point. She started swimming. Not too fast, she prayed. Not too slow, she hoped.

Pausing at the usual distance, she raised the camera with her right hand. With her left, she lifted all four fingers pressed tightly together, her thumb pressed flat against her palm.

Unblinkingly, Vegas responded. Four right-side tentacles up, then down. Remembering to breathe, she checked the camera she had not had occasion to use in many weeks. In the viewfinder a small red light winked steadily back at her, like the eye of the Devil.

Dead battery.

A good scientist always, always travels with backup. Hurriedly placing the useless unit back into its pouch on her vest, she removed the second camera. A quick check showed it was half powered: more than enough. Turning back to the hovering cuttlefish, she made the goodbye gesture once again. It was not mimicked.

She tried several times more before she noticed that the always fluttering, flowing lateral fins were not moving. The camera lowered. Finning forward, she reached out with her free hand. She had never touched Vegas before; had never tried to make physical contact for fear of frightening him off. It was her experience that cuttlefish did not like to be touched. But there was no objection, no retreat, as she first lightly made contact with the heavy body, then ran her open palm along its ventral side. She pushed, gently. The body started to float away. Already its healthy reddish-orange color was beginning to fade. The eyes, of course, remained open and visible; just not moving. Realization made her swallow hard. She could—she *would*—continue her research. There was no way she could cease it now. Even though she would have to start all over again with another subject. Next time with a younger one.

Vegas truly had been saying goodbye.

13

Valentin Sharffen and the Code of Doom

The longest story in this collection has the shortest introduction.

Advances in artificial intelligence have greatly enhanced the gaming experience.

Mightn't the reverse also be true?

—I—

The battle was on the verge of becoming a complete rout, until Sharffen appeared.

Streaked with blood, frightened, and exhausted, Lieutenant Polan felt as if he had run into a brick wall. Steadying himself, he looked up to see it was only another soldier. Then he noticed the twin stars on the front of the tall man's helmet. Explosions and the whoosh of powerful slip-strainers echoing in his ears, he blinked away grime and sweat. This was most unusual. Exceptional, even. Soldiers didn't see generals on the field, much less those sporting two stars.

Six foot four, trim as an Olympic swimmer, the unexpected arrival scanned the scarred field of battle behind Polan. The senior officer's face had been hacked and chiseled as if by a sculptor who had been working with only one good eye and a permanent chip on his shoulder. Polan found himself transfixed by deep-set eyes that were the blackest he had ever seen. Black as obsidian, black as a seam of fresh coal, black as deep space itself. Bottomless and impenetrable.

After taking the measure of the chaotic battlefield, they looked down at him.

"Where are your superior officers, Lieutenant …?"

"Polan, sir." The younger man fought to straighten and salute. "Dead, sir. All of them. Or mortally wounded."

A Durgeon splinter shell landed close by, sending hundreds of metal shards screaming behind the two men and shredding a pair of small trees. While the Lieutenant ducked instinctively, the general did not so much as flinch. The shrieks and wails of dying men and women sintered the cracks in the cacophony of combat. Polan dropped to the ground as a second shell came whistling in their direction. Above him, the general's gaze narrowed as he tracked it with his eyes. Something big and nasty went *whomp* nearby, precipitating a geyser of dirt, macerated wood, and less savory debris. The bone sticking out of a lacerated wrist, a human hand waxed with gore landed on the senior officer's right shoulder. Reaching up, he brushed it away without so much as looking at it.

"Get up, Polan." The younger man complied, struggling out of the clinging muck. "You're Captain Polan now." With a sweep of the same palm that had indifferently shucked off the dismembered hand, the two-star indicated the field of battle. "I am General Valentin Sharffen and I'm taking command here. Get on your communicator. Organize a defensive line. Bring the disorganized together, but keep falling back as you do so. Have your noncoms stay in touch. We'll have a retreat, but not a panic. Let the Durgeon continue to advance, make them think they've won."

Polan swallowed. So much death left no time for tact. "I think maybe they have … sir."

Sharffen growled. "I disagree. Not all the guts in this Corps have been left on the field. Not yet." His gaze flicked to another soldier who was limping toward them. The woman's left arm was shredded and had been hurriedly patched with sealskin, but her expression was alert. "You. Who are you?"

The woman glanced at Polan, then back at the General. Her left eye was nearly swollen shut from some unknown impact. "Captain Louise Sanchez, sir."

"Major Sanchez, I see that your field comm unit is intact. Where's our armor?"

She nodded past him, in the same direction she and Polan had been running. "Ahead of us, sir."

Sharffen shook his head once, sharply. "You mean behind us. That's wrong. Get on your comm. Tell whoever's left in charge to swing everything that's still capable of combat toward Marsters Gorge. About four kilometers in there's a side canyon that turns north. Always foggy in there, and full of active thermal vents. Fog will mask visual and the vents will confuse the enemy's heat-seekers. If our people take that they can get behind the Durgeon lines. Tell them to move their ennervar-plated butts, and wait for my command to counterattack." He looked back at Polan. "Their ground forces will keep pushing us westward. We'll bleed them until our armor is behind them." His enunciation was sharp enough to cut granite. "Then we'll hit them with everything we've got."

Strength Polan believed had left him now began to return. This strange and unannounced senior officer inspired not just hope, but confidence. "I'm on it, sir!" He stumbled away and pulled his communicator, intent on systematizing the organized retreat the general had requested. The newly promoted Major was less hopeful.

"Excuse me, sir, but our heavy armor will never make it through Marsters. That route was surveyed and discarded prior to this battle and rejected as being too narrow for tanks and mobile launchers."

Sharffen nodded, having anticipated the objection. "Not if our launchers go first. Make sure each one has a field engineer with the crew. If the launchers hug the canyon wall, their integral repression fields will flatten out the old road that runs through the canyon. That will clear enough space for heavy armor to follow. The Durgeon won't be expecting such a thrust any more than you did. When our armor hits them from behind, our ground forces will have regrouped enough to hit back hard." Raising one gnarled hand, he clenched it into a fist. "We'll squeeze them, Major, and they'll break."

Incredible, she thought through the pain in what was left of her arm. Who was this officer? Why had she never heard his name before? As unabashed on the battlefield as Polan had been, she asked him as much.

"I was just assigned to this sector, Major. Good thing, too, from what I've seen so far. Now get on your comm and tell our armor they're going the wrong way!"

"Yes *sir*!" Buoyed by his energy and assurance, she started making the necessary calls.

Catastrophe, Sharffen thought to himself. What a ghastly mess. Well, he'd fix it. If the troops falling back could regroup long enough to slow the Durgeon advance before they were pushed into the river Lissum, they'd surprise the hell out of the invaders. Earth didn't need any more losses in the field. More than territory was at stake here, he knew. The Terran defenses needed bolstering emotionally as well as physically, and he was just the man to do it.

That was when the sun disappeared, and everything stopped.

Another man, any other man, would have been staggered. By the abruptness of it all. By the overwhelming totality. Would have fallen to his knees and covered his eyes in fear. It did not just go dark: the sun literally vanished. Around Sharffen, nothing moved. Not a bird, not a scavenging canine: nothing. Frowning, he started forward. Within moments he had encountered a decimated platoon of retreating troops. Motionless as statues, their expressions frozen in fear or concern or contemplation, they stood where they had been stopped. Reaching out, he felt of necks and chests. There was no movement. No pulsing of veins, no beating of hearts. Yet they did not appear to be dead. Only petrified.

What the hell was this? he wondered.

His first thought, naturally, was that the invading Durgeon had unleashed some new weapon. Some kind of raybeam that produced instant paralysis. But what could that have to do with the disappearance of the sun? Continuing onward, his progress illuminated by a dim glow whose source he could not discern but for which he was inordinately grateful, he encountered more and more fleeing soldiers and occasionally their mechanized transport. All were stilled in place. Nothing moved around him, not even a forlorn butterfly.

That was when he had the idea.

The skid lay where it had stopped, brought to a halt when it had been abandoned. Its operator, a corporal, lay decapitated in a ditch nearby, the wide open eyes of his guillotined head gazing toward eternity. Stepping onto the personal transport, Sharffen spoke to the ignition. It ignored him and refused to start up until he used the senior officer override built into his own communicator. Upon accepting the necessary sequence it rose silently beneath him. Entering the desired coordinates as best he could remember them, he checked to make sure the energy level of the slenderslicer mounted on the front of the skid held at least half a charge before he gave the command to accelerate. Directly toward the enemy lines.

Given the pace at which the humans had been retreating he did not expect much time to elapse before he encountered the first Durgeon troops. Sure enough, a cluster of them soon hove into view. Bipedal, bisymmetrical, scaled, and vaguely Piscean in appearance, their bulbous skulls and flaring armor made them stand out from the surrounding dark and devastated terrain. Bending slightly forward, Sharffen prepared to let loose with the slicer.

That was when he noticed that they were as locked in place as the troops he had left behind.

Slowing the skid, riding its repellers half a meter above the torn-up ground, he soared past them. Not a one turned slitted eyes in his direction. Not a weapon swung around to bear on the intrusive human target. The light here was as bad as that behind him, the sun just as absent. The reality of the situation came crashing home without the need for additional verification.

In all the world, or at least this corner of it, General Valentin Sharffen was the only thing that moved.

Absorbing the monstrous totality of his motionless surroundings he flew onward until eventually he reached his objective: the Durgeon field headquarters. Drawing his sidearm as he hopped off the hovering skid, he made his way past ranks of waiting alien soldiers, past blast doors that were halfway open, down a shielded tunnel, until at last he found himself in the inner sanctum. Intimately familiar as he was with Durgeon devices, within moments he was standing beside the commanding alien officer. The High Marshal was staring at a float screen that showed the field of battle: position of ground forces, armor, artillery, the topographic layout, and much more.

Raising his pistol, Sharffen placed the end of the muzzle against the side of the Marshal's head, just between the two fin-like auditory organs that flared from the left side of the skull. It would only take him a minute to assassinate the Marshal and his entire staff. Sharffen could take his time, striding around the command center while eliminating them one by one. His finger tensed on the trigger. Start with the Marshal and then … and then …

He hesitated, pondering. The urge to follow through, to kill, was powerful within him. Powerful, but not quite overpowering. Sharffen prided himself on being a soldier who could grasp the *entire* field of battle, much as a chessmaster might analyze the board before him and the position of the pieces upon it. More than a little was happening that made no sense. Taking out the Durgeon senior staff made sense, yes, but only in the context of everything else making sense. Which, he was starting to think, it did not.

Lowering the pistol, he rested it on his lap as he sat down in an oversized alien chair to wait for some sense to return.

HE WAS AWAKENED from having dozed off by the return of sound and movement around him. As if nothing had happened, the Durgeon resumed everything they had been doing before the paralysis had struck. Tacticians poured over their readouts and screens, assistants strode purposefully through the command chamber, others argued in their high-pitched, rapid-fire speech.

Needless to say, recognition of his presence was met with a combination of fear and shock.

He sat calmly as half a dozen weapons were hastily drawn and aimed in his direction. Listening to the confused chatter that now surrounded him, he was almost amused. Another time he might have enjoyed their panic. Not now. Not when something greater than immediate success in battle was at stake. What had happened to the sun, for example. Having finished first in class in Durgeon speech studies, he had no difficulty understanding what was being said around him.

"You can shoot me any time you wish," he finally interjected. Immediately, discussion ceased in his vicinity. They were clearly surprised and startled by his fluency. "I would ask that you first hear me out."

It was the Marshal himself (Sharffen decided to reference it as a "him," as the Durgeon were not gender-specific) who approached.

"I am Culd-ad-Culm, Commander of the Fourth Force." Wide,

bulging eyes took the measure of the impossible intruder. "I detect that you are a twice-general officer. Your presence here is inexplicable. I do not understand." A flexible three-fingered hand indicated the surrounding arc of equally fish-eyed subordinates. "None of us comprehend. How did you get in here? Have your kind mastered teleportation?"

"That would be easier to understand than what has actually happened." Feeling no fear, Sharffen displayed none. His striking presence and confidence was no more lost on the aliens than they had been on his own troops.

He proceeded to explain what he had experienced in the course of the preceding day. Disbelief was universal, as he knew it would be. Just as he knew he had only one viable card to play.

"If I am hallucinating all this, then nothing will come of it. I will become your prisoner, to do with as you wish. If, on the other hand, similar circumstances should recur, as I suspect they might, then I will find a way to prove it to you."

The Marshal gestured his comprehension. "You realize, surely, that regardless of whether your incredible elucidation proves to have any basis in reality or not, you can never leave this place alive."

Sharffen's expression betrayed no feeling. "If I am wrong, then you are right. If I am right, then our lives may mean nothing anyway. Give me two days."

Culd-ad-Culm's huge eyes rolled in their sockets like glycerin-slickened ball bearings. "In two days we will have driven your surviving soldiers to the bank of the great river, and the battle will be over."

"If I am right," Sharffen replied tersely, "in two days we may all be over."

IT DID NOT TAKE two days. According to Sharffen's communicator, less than one had passed when the paralysis struck again. As for himself, he felt nothing. Not a tingle, not a shock, not a moment of inexplicable disorientation. Nothing. But around him, all movement ceased and the light dimmed. From High Marshal Culd-ad-Culm down to the lowliest member of the Durgeon fighting order, motion ceased. The battle screens froze, indicators ceased functioning. Everything simply—stopped.

Rising from the seat where he had been ordered to remain, he walked slowly around the Marshal and a pair of his subalterns. Picking up first the Marshal, who weighed less than the average human male, he carried him out of the command chamber and through the access tunnel before finally lying him down gently beside a refuse tank. Returning to the room he repeated the action one at a time with three of the Marshal's staff, positioning them beside each other. Recovering the pistol that had been taken from him, he added a Durgeon sidearm from an unresponsive subofficer before walking back outside. Then he settled down to wait. Adding to the enveloping strangeness, he did not feel tired nor any need to sleep.

As before, the return of movement, sound, and light awoke him. To his credit, Culd-ad-Culm was the first not only to awake but to attempt an evaluation of the incomprehensible.

"Here." Having displayed his ownership of both weapons, Sharffen proceeded to pass them back to his enemies. Still stunned, one of the Marshal's subordinates accepted them, fully realizing the import of the human's gesture.

Utterly bewildered, another asked, "How did we get out here?"

"I carried you." Sharffen nodded back toward the entrance to the command bunker. Startled soldiers were talking among themselves and gesturing in the direction of their superiors, who were slowly awakening and trying to make sense of what had happened to them. Sharffen continued.

"I brought you outside, arranged you on the ground, and took the two guns simply to show that I could have killed you without effort."

"But you did not." The alien commander was staring at him. "Why did you not?"

General Valentin Sharffen's voice was grim. "Because I think we are engaged in a three-way battle with a mutual enemy that is unseen and unidentified, and if we do not join forces or at the very least forge some kind of a truce, that in the end we will both be annihilated."

"Aw, man!"

Tyrone leaned toward the screen. No doubt about it: the image was frozen. Before checking with Lewis, he tried several tried and true techniques for unfreezing the action. None of them worked. Adjusting the pickup mike that looped downward from his headphones, he spoke to his friend.

"Lew, I'm all jammed up here."

The reply was a surprise but not a shock. "You too? I thought it was only at my end. Just happened. You tried unfreeze, save and restart, different battle screen?"

"All of the above." His frustrated friend leaned back slightly in his chair. His room was small but cozy and when he was into what was on screen, he felt it doubled in size. "Man, I don't wanna reboot! Stuff was just hotting up!"

"*You* don't want to reboot?" Lewis' voice was arch with frustration. "I was kicking your ass! You think *I* want to reboot?"

"I was just reassembling my forces," a defensive Tyrone muttered back.

"Sure you were." His friend's smugness came through plainly. "On top of all your dead bodies. Seriously though, man, I don't think we have a choice."

Tyrone sighed as his fingers moved toward the keyboard. "Fuck it, then. I'm saving." A brief pause. "Rebooting now."

While his machine shut down and restarted, he considered the possibilities. None of them were encouraging. Hopefully the freeze was just the result of a one-time, undefined glitch. It wasn't impossible. If that was the case, in the end all it would cost them was some game time. He liked playing against Lewis. His friend was an excellent tactician and knew pretty much everything there was to know about the game. His weakness was a reluctance to commit sufficient forces to go for a swift kill. In their head-to-head competitions, they were running about even. When they combined to play the MMU version of the game they usually stomped all over their opponents. Even the gang from Seoul.

It did not take long for his souped-up machine to flash ready. Reloading the game, Tyrone was pleased to see that it had returned to the exact spot where play had frozen. Well, maybe he wasn't entirely pleased. Despite what he had said, there was no question that Lewis, who was directing the Durgeon this time, was well ahead on body count as well as battlefield position. Without waiting for his friend to acknowledge that he had reloaded and hoping to gain a few meters of battleground, Tyrone eagerly gripped his joystick and prepared to move a squad of demolition experts toward an as-yet-incomplete alien turret emplacement.

The joystick moved, but the figures depicted did not move. The screen remained frozen. Sitting back, he slapped the arms of his chair hard and muttered "Shit!" The still-connected Lewis hailed him via the headphones.

"I heard that. Double it for me."

"You still froze up too?"

"Yeah. What the hell, man?"

His co-player took a deep breath. "Virus?"

"Can't be." Tyrone could almost see Lewis, who lived on the other side of town, shaking his head. "I've got every antivirus program you can think of on my machine, plus double firewalls. Not even my student loan coordinator can get through without raising two or three pop-up alerts."

"Pretty much the same here." Tyrone's anger subsided as his curiosity intensified. "Can't be a Trojan, either. For the same reasons. Wonder if Gcube is doing an unannounced update?"

"Shouldn't do that without telling players they'll be interrupting gameplay," Lewis responded, referring to the name of the game company. "Still, I suppose it's not unprecedented. I'm going to …"

"… check my machine," Tyrone finished for him. He was already entering commands.

Relief was forthcoming. "You were right, bro. That's all it is. Don't know why the game should freeze just to acquire a new character, though. Should be able to continue play while the upgrade downloads."

"It's your character," Lewis shot back. "Human soldier. I've got him in my file, too."

Studying the sidebar, Tyrone read aloud. "Valentin Sharffen. Major General, United Planetary Defense Forces. Born Yekaterinberg, Russia. Height six-four, weight 220. Graduated first in class Tactics, first in class Global Strategics, second in class Gunnery, first in class … this character's a bit much, Lew. I'm looking for the usual counter-programmed faults and I'm not seeing any."

His friend had a reasonable comeback. "Maybe they're down-loading him to you in the hopes that he can save your ugly butt. Going to take more than one senior officer to resist the Durgeon tide, though."

"That so? Let's see. I'll try engaging him via Direct Field Command."

Once again, nothing worked. The screen, and the game, remained unresponsive.

"Crap, crap, *crap!*" Tyrone would've hit the keyboard if he'd thought it would have done any good. "I'm still dead here."

"Me too. Look, maybe it's a new kind of trojan."

"What kind of trojan *resists* you installing it?" Tyrone snapped.

"I don't know. I'm a gamer, not a black hacker. The game was working perfectly until this new character was downloaded, or uploaded, or whatever. Right now I'm thinking if we delete him we can get back to where we were."

Tyrone considered. "Why not just go back and do a general restore, from yesterday?"

"Might not get rid of the install," Lewis countered. "Or it might work and we'd find ourselves back at this same point all over again, still froze up."

"Fine, fine." Anxious to resume play, Tyrone was ready to try anything. He moved the gun cursor over the new character bar. "Let's do it together, then. One, two … delete." He entered the necessary control sequence.

There was a very bright flash and a muffled snapping sound. It crackled throughout the two-story suburban house, reaching far enough and loud enough to distract the woman in the kitchen from her dinner preparations. Wiping her hands with a dish towel, she called out toward the back of the building.

"Tyrone? Tyrone, you okay back there? You're not messin' around with that fake laser again, are you? Tyrone!"

That boy, she thought as she put the towel down on the counter and headed for his room. Why couldn't he get himself with something sensible, like football or girls, instead of sitting staring at that computer all day? Boy didn't get enough sunshine, let alone exercise.

His door was closed, as usual. Unusually, a strong acrid smell was sifting through from the other side.

"Tyrone! I told you that if you were gonna keep smokin' that stuff you needed to do it …"

Her voice broke off as she opened the door. Her boy, pride of the freshman class at the nearby college, was lying on his back on the floor. His eyes were wide open. So was his mouth. Smoke rose from the blackened, carbonized tip of his right forefinger. He was not moving. First she screamed, then she ran back to the kitchen to dial 911, knocking over two hallway tables and a standing lamp in the process.

The call to the lawyers came later.

The scandal was sizeable, the payouts considerable. As a result of the defective game-cum-console, three deaths in total were attributable to the still unresolved anomaly. Tyrone Landsford and Lewis Chang in Los Angeles, and a continent away and fifteen minutes later, valedictorian and bound-for-Yale high school senior Martin Goldberg of Brooklyn Heights, New York.

Gcube reacted about as quickly as could be expected, given the unprecedented and incomprehensible nature of the problem. Just not quickly enough, the vampirish pundits declared, to prevent the deaths of three talented and promising young men.

Even though no one else died or was injured, the online version of Durgeon Invasion: Part IV was simply wiped from existence as rapidly as possible. Though it cost the gaming company a bundle, they really had no other choice. Besides, the financial hit was nothing compared to the PR disaster. Whether they continued gameplay harmlessly or not, all physical copies of the game were immediately remotely disabled, followed by instructions that they should be deleted from their hosting hard drives in lieu of a potential life-threatening hazard. Double refunds were promised. Gcube was big enough that it could survive the blow.

Having thus performed damage control to the best of their ability, the company execs desperately needed to know what had happened.

The manufacturer of the console was quickly cleared of any responsibility. Every other game that had been built for their machine played as designed. There were no adverse consequences, no hidden dangers. Only Durgeon Invasion: Part IV had somehow compromised the console's electronics to the point where the keyboards used by the trio of deceased players had caused a lethal jolt of electricity to shoot through their young bodies. The possibility of something like it happening had been discussed, discreetly, throughout the industry for many, many years. Decades, even. But the prospect had never advanced beyond a far-fetched theoretical possibility. No one had actually, seriously believed that a computer keyboard or joystick could carry enough juice to electrocute a person even if that individual was resting all ten fingers on a board that was sopping wet.

Finding out what had happened was not going to be easy. The keyboards and computers of Landsford and Chang had been thoroughly fried, their hard drives slagged. But while Goldberg's machine had similarly caught fire, his older sister had retained enough presence of mind to douse it with the contents of a family fire extinguisher. It was badly impacted, but maybe not irretrievably so.

That was the hope, anyway, of the two company engineers who were busy making final connections to the hard drive they had resurrected from the blackened machine. If they could recover all the information leading up to the fatal electrical discharge, they might learn what had happened—and why.

Annalee made the final connection, then walked back around the wide work bench to lean over Roget's left shoulder. "Power it up, Paul. Take it real slow."

"How would I know to do anything," he muttered as the middle of the three big flat screens that formed a semicircle on his desk came to life in front of him, "without you around to tell me?"

"Sorry. Pardon me if I'm just a little nervous."

"No reason to be nervous," he chided her. "Anything untoward starts to happen, any kind of serious surge, it will automatically trip all power to the test bed the instant it manifests itself. Which won't help us learn what happened, but will protect your makeup."

She pinched his ear. Lightly. Roget was a little bit of a man, and a little bit of a genius. Not a loins-melting combination, but not wholly unattractive, either. It suited her that he was a coworker much more than a potential date. They worked well together.

"Game is coming up," he murmured. She shunted casual musings aside as, all business now, she concentrated her full attention on the screen.

There was nothing remarkable about the image that solidified. It was a standard screen shot from the game, one of thousands of similar visual options written into the Durgeon Invasion program. Soldiers dying, smoke rising, trees falling. Except that this particular scene was the last one that had appeared on Martin Goldberg's computer monitor the instant before his death. Had Tyrone Landsford and Lewis Chang also died while viewing the same game screen?

An uncharacteristically tense Annalee checked the left and right monitors. "Console power consumption is normal. Absolutely normal. No sign of a spike, contained or imminent."

"Let's play, then." Roget grasped the linked joystick that was no different from the standard store-bought one that came with this particular iteration of the gaming console and proceeded to manipulate it with one hand while hitting keys and buttons with the other. This continued for some ten minutes before he called a halt and looked back up at her.

"There's nothing amiss here. If this unit hadn't been pulled from a burning computer you'd never know there was anything wrong with it. The game progresses normally." He turned back to the screen. "I can play, switch sides, or play against the machine." He shook his head tersely. "I don't see anything wrong with either the game or the console."

"Neither did Martin Goldberg," she murmured, "before he was electrocuted."

"At least we have it narrowed down." Roget pressed his left fore-finger to his lips as he speculated aloud. "Three teens died while playing this game. Everyone else continued to play it until it was shut down or otherwise disabled. What made those three different?"

"Parents didn't pay their electrical bills?" she suggested coolly.

"Very funny." He sat up straight. "We're going to have to go through the whole game bit by bit, screen by screen, from the begin-ning, exploring all the options in order to ..."

"Paul, do you know how *many* options Durgeon Invasion: Part IV has?"

"I know, I know. But I don't see any other way. We've already run an incongruity search on unburned copies of the game and found nothing. So we're going to have rerun the scan manually on this copy, one option at a time. Each character, each battlefield scenario, each device, even the weather in the game. *Something* triggered those lethal electrical blowbacks. The company needs to know what it was."

"Not to mention the company's legal department." She walked to a nearby desk. Like Roget's it was overflowing with components. "You start on that one and I'll launch a fresh copy over here."

THEY WERE at it for days, picking apart Durgeon Invasion: Part IV from D to V. Breaks from work were full of jokes, cold pastry, and strong coffee as they discussed anything but their current project. Periodic nervous memos from Corporate were ignored: their work could not be rushed. After the first week, Company stopped pestering them. Annalee had briskly assured their anxious superiors that results would be announced as soon as they had any to announce.

They were four-fifths of the way through the game, having processed thousands of options, and had arrived close to the point where the unexplained electrical faults had occurred, when a frowning Roget looked over from his desk and announced to his colleague almost apologetically, "Annalee, I think I might have something here."

She was out of her chair and at his side immediately. He could have ported his discovery over to her, of course, but since they actually worked side-by-side in the office it was one of those uncommon circumstances in contemporary tech where actual physical person-to-person communication was able to function more efficiently than the electronic variety.

Standing behind him she bent close to stare at the middle of the three oversized monitors. "What've you got, Paul?"

"Probably nothing," he told her with typical modesty. "It's a small abnormality. On the face of it, it seems harmless enough. In fact, it involves a face. But it's still an anomaly. At least I think it is."

She frowned. "What do you mean, 'you think it is'? Either it's an anomaly or it's not."

"One would think so, wouldn't one? Even if it meets the criteria we're looking for, I still don't see how it could have anything to do with or how it could trigger a serious, let alone lethal, electrical fault in the console itself." Sitting back and folding his small hands over his stomach, he gestured at the screen.

Annalee scrutinized the sidebar. It was a typical character sidebar, one that popped up whenever the gamer selected a new individual to put in play. The character design was appropriately detailed, the uniformed image facing outward properly martial.

Valentin Sharffen. Rank: Major General. History ...

It took her about a minute to process the entire character description: longer than usual because the character had a resume that was more extensive than average. That was to be expected for the character background of a senior officer. It was written in standard DA game prose, straightforward and without embellishment. She was troubled by it before she had finished reading.

"I know every character in the game, all four versions, including those designed to end up as dead bodies within five minutes of play." She shook her head. "I don't recognize this one."

"Neither do I." Raising his left hand to rest it against his chin, Roget squinted at the center monitor. "But there it is. Full background, all the usual appurtenances." Swiveling his chair, he indicated the monitor off to his right. "And there's the applicable code. I've highlighted it in red. Fully developed, no glitches." Tilting his head back, he looked up at her. "Seems like a nice, useful, charismatic character. There's just one problem with it."

She nodded slowly. "We didn't develop him. Gcube has nothing to do with him. He's entirely new to me."

"And me. So we have an impossible game-related triple fatality, and in the game scenario at least one of the three dead kids was playing, a character who shouldn't be there." He smiled thinly. "Suggests possibilities, wouldn't you say?"

She pursed her lips. "Unavoidably. But what kind, and how? Durgeon Invasion isn't open source. Even if Goldberg or all three of those boys had the combined talent of three of the best programmers in the world, they wouldn't have had access to the development code, and they wouldn't have known how or where to start. A trio of geniuses might have been able to formulate the character, but they couldn't have ported him into the game. You can't tether a program to one that doesn't accept external modification."

"What about somebody inside the company? Somebody in Gcube development?" Roget hypothesized.

She considered. "Sure. A programmer with too much time on their hands could have built the character, coded it, and pushed it out as an upgrade or an add-on. But that doesn't explain why a straightforward single-character upgrade would cause the gaming console to deliver a fatal electrical charge to a trio of total strangers." Hesitation altered her tone. "Unless our theoretical rogue programmer is a psychotic murderer."

Roget fidgeted in his chair. "We don't know what those kids were doing that might have caused the problem. If a rogue programmer inside the company pushed the upgrade, it might have gone to hundreds of consoles. The recall came immediately after the three fatalities." He glanced up again. "I'm supposing that none of the other players managed to duplicate the action, the necessary sequence of events within the game, that caused our trio of deaths. Maybe there was something about the dead boys' multiplayer gameplay at that particular moment and in that particular instant of the game that generated the problem. Or maybe our rogue programmer only pushed his new character code to a few consoles."

She was pacing behind him now. "What if there is no rogue programmer? What if the game itself generated the character? You know it has the ability to do that, to advance gameplay in unexpected and unanticipated ways. It's part of what makes—what made—Durgeon Invasion such a best seller." Halting, she indicated his center monitor. "But I've never seen a game-generated character this fully developed. Usually they're just loosely described cannon fodder. And that still doesn't explain why or how just inserting a new character into the game caused the electrical problem. We upgrade DA with new characters and battlefield scenarios on a regular basis. What's so special and/or dangerous about this piece of code?" Advancing, she leaned over to squint at the brightly lit screen. "Admittedly this is an initial, cursory look-over, but I don't see anything radical embedded in the sequence. It looks like clear-cut character code to me."

Roget nodded. "Same here. When we break it down maybe we'll find something unusual." He gestured at the monitor. "First step is to see how the game plays without the unauthorized new character." The finger on his right hand knew where the Delete button was without him having to glance at the keyboard.

"Don't do that, civilian."

Paul Roget had been in the gaming business for more than ten years. He had seen much, presided over important developments, been on panels that postulated possible future innovations for the industry. So had Annalee Henshaw. But this was the first time their jaws had dropped at anything they had seen on a monitor, and they dropped in unison.

"Holy mother of motherboards." Roget was unaware he was whispering.

"Characters are programmed to respond verbally to player input." His colleague murmured softly as she stared wide-eyed at the monitor. "The only programming I can recall that can produce a negative involves battlefield maneuvering and choices. It doesn't come up—it can't come up—in response to a perceived physical gesture on the part of the gamer. Kinetics are reserved for battlefield play on the part of the players."

"There is no 'play' on a battlefield, civilian." The character voice was rich, deep, and sharp. Accusatory, even, a dumbfounded Roget thought.

"Oh, now that tears it," Annalee mumbled. "That just screws it upside down and inside out and sideways." She was shaking her head in disbelief. "The character exhibits independent volition outside the preprogrammed auditory parameters." Taking a step forward, she reached for the Delete herself.

"I am formally advising you not to touch that button, ma'am."

Her hand hesitated above the keyboard, her disbelief now magnified by a factor of ten. "Is that …? Are you *threatening* me?"

"Christ," Roget muttered, "now the game threatens a player?" His brows drew together. "Wait a minute. How is he—how is it—even perceiving us? In real time, no less?"

She nodded in the direction of the left-hand monitor. "Built-in cameras are on."

Roget swallowed hard. "I didn't activate that app." His gaze returned to the stern-visaged character on the center screen. "This is fucking crazy. If you weren't here, I'd be on my way to Urgent Care right now. Maybe we both should go anyway."

"Maybe we should." Her voice was grim. "But first …" Her right hand started to descend toward the keyboard anew, index finger extended.

"Final warning, ma'am." The character was staring straight out at them. At me, Roget wondered? At her?

"Or what?" she snapped back. *Jesus Christ, I'm arguing with a computer character.*

"Just—don't—do it."

"Screw this." She hit Delete.

There was an overpowering flash of light followed by several flares of lesser and rapidly diminishing intensity. Loud crackling filled the room, followed by smoke that issued from the localized server. Roget was knocked back off his chair. Annalee let out a muffled scream, clutched at her right hand, and crumpled to the floor. A moment later the overhead fire suppression system came on, knocking down the incipient blaze from the server, the three monitors, the pair of keyboards, and attendant devices, all of which were sparking, smoking, or in flames. Rising from the floor and blinking away water that continued to waterfall from the ceiling sprinklers, the analyst sought his companion through the smoke and spray.

"Annalee. Annalee!"

She was sitting on the floor, soaked, her short black hair plastered against her head and neck, holding her right wrist with her left hand. Several dark streaks showed where she had been burned. She was starting to tremble.

He helped her to her feet. "We need to get you to the First Aid station, have that looked at."

She stared up at him, shocked in several ways, none of them comprehensible except the physical. "It—he hurt me. He *hurt* me."

"Rogue program." Putting his arm around her, he helped her up and guided her toward the hallway door. The sounds of rising commotion were starting to reach them from outside. Steve Phelps burst into the room, wielding a fire extinguisher like a short-barreled gun.

"Paul, Annalee, what the …?" He broke off, staring not at the damage but at her. "What the hell happened to your hand?"

Roget eased her past the engineer, out into the hall, and through the rapidly gathering crowd of baffled colleagues. "We're okay," he said reassuringly. He kept repeating it as he and Annalee made their way down the corridor. "We're okay."

"Hardware safeties." There was the faintest edge of panic in her voice. "Built-in security." She met his concerned gaze. "Otherwise we'd be as dead as those three poor boys."

"I wonder." He led her around a corner. "Were they engaged in the same scenario? Were they also trying to delete the character profile?"

"We may never know. Maybe they were. Maybe it was something

else." Her voice strengthened and there was a glint in her eyes. "I do know one thing. Every returned copy of Durgeon Invasion: Part IV gets scanned before it gets recycled. If that character code is in all of them, then we have a potential ongoing problem."

"What are we going to do about online downloads?" he muttered.

"We can push out a general remote delete. Without any—personal interaction—I don't think removing that character code should provoke a ..."

She couldn't say it, so he did so for her. "An individualized response?" She nodded. "Maybe only a few gamers running multi-player play got the code, or utilized it in the specific kind of sequence that would cause it to engage. Maybe only them—and us. It might not be as wide a problem as we fear." They were almost to the First Aid office. Someone had called ahead and the duty nurse was standing in the hall looking anxiously in their direction.

"It better not be." She winced as she lowered her burned hand, careful not to make contact with the wall. "Meanwhile you and I and the whole rest of the Gcube team have a lot of work ahead of us trying to find out exactly where that code originated."

"Or how," he finished as he pushed the door open.

Devin turned up the volume and adjusted his headset, trying to snug it tighter against his ears. Crapon (his stepfather's real name was Carpon, but Devin never thought of him as that: he was and would always be Crapon) was beating on his mother again. Wasn't the first time, wouldn't be the last. All Devin could do was try to drown out the noise and pretend he didn't hear the confrontation. If he tried to inter-cede on his mother's behalf, his stepfather would turn his booze-fired rage on her son instead. Reaching up, he felt of the knot on the back of his head. It had gone down quite a bit since Crapon had thrown him into the refrigerator, but there was still a noticeable bump. Devin had no wish to reinvigorate it.

A crash came from the vicinity of the kitchen. His mother was throwing dishes at her third husband, or else he was taking them out of the cupboard and smashing them against the floor out of spite. Good. If the sonofabitch was breaking dishes, then he wasn't hitting his mother. Devin turned the volume up as far as he could stand it.

It was a sorry testament to the debasement of what passed for a home life that he found the rage and fury of synthetic battle more calming than the usual household background noise. The game restarted where he had left off, but before he could engage play he was interrupted by a pop-up. He didn't bother to read it, wiping it from the screen with a keyboard touch. The contents were identical to the pop-ups he and his friends who had the same game had been receiving for more than a week. A standard anti-virus safety upgrade, the pop-ups declaimed. Downloaded and installed automatically, without the need for action by the gamer. He made a rude noise. *How many times were they going to have to run the upgrade?* he asked himself.

He shrugged. The pause was brief and insofar as he could tell did not in any way affect gameplay. His friends Colton and Bophan and Marie, with whom he often multiplayed, had suffered through the same string of repetitive upgrades and likewise had reported no perceptible changes. Colton and Marie were running the Durgeon version IV offense while he and Bophan maneuvered the Terran defense forces. Over the past couple of months their two-way combat had shifted back and forth. Sometimes the Colton-Marie Durgeon forces were in the ascendant, other days and weeks it was the Devin-Bophan fighting machine that came close, but could not quite manage, to push the heinous invaders off the planet.

He smiled to himself. Unbeknownst to that sometimes supercilious Colton and know-it-all (but really kinda pretty) Marie, their wily opponent had an ace up his sleeve. Or rather, a flash drive.

Removing it from the drawer of his battered, second-hand desk, he slid it into an open port. Re-activating the game, he hit OFF-LINE PLAY and waited while the flash drive booted up. Wary of his mother, hating his stepfather, uncertain about his teachers, he had learned long ago to trust no one. That distrust extended to and included everyone he had ever met (except Colton and Bophan and probably Marie, even though she was a girl). It did not exclude the authors of the textbooks he was required to read, the presenters on the television and web news, nor even the manufacturers of the games to which he fled and in which he loved to lose himself whenever anarchy descended upon his home. Distrust had kept him safe.

He felt of the back of his head and winced. In his house, safe was never more than a relative term.

So when Gcube announced they were running a full recall on unused copies of Durgeon Invasion: Part IV, and pushing out a safety upgrade to those already in the hands of consumers, he was immediately suspicious. Other games had done "safety" upgrades and recalls because some clutch of distraught mothers had objected to a particularly bloody sequence, or one that pushed the boundaries of R-ratedness, or featured a character whose design, or morals, or actions to which they objected. Having been forced to learn at a preternatural age how to make hard decisions in his life, Devin was not about to let some faraway computer company make decisions for him where his gaming was concerned. So, just in case, before the first safety upgrade could be pushed to his console, he had saved the game he had been playing to a separate, isolated drive.

As soon as its contents had been re-installed on his computer, he hit Resume for the game. Colton and Marie were still off-line and Bophan wouldn't be home from his part-time job for another hour. That gave Devin more than enough time to see whether the alterations the Gcube people wanted him to install for the latest version of the game were actually to his benefit or to theirs. All of his critical material—schoolwork, serious gameplay, his private diary—were safely ensconced on other password protected flash drives as well as on his out-of-date but still serviceable laptop, which was not connected to the internet. A third set of his vitals resided in the cloud. So even if something went seriously wrong with his unaltered version of Durgeon Invasion: Part IV and went so far as to damage his computer, everything else was isolated and safe.

And if it killed his computer, he could reiterate his frequent plea for a new one.

The familiar Durgeon Invasion opening screen appeared. A couple of keyboard clicks shot him past the most excellent but long since viewed and memorized opening CGI sequence, whereupon without further delay he found himself back on the most recent battlefield. This one was set somewhere in the South Pacific, among volcanic islands and involving exciting underwater play. Here, Colton and Marie had gotten the upper hand over him and Bophan, but neither of them knew that Devin and his partner were secretly marshalling a flotilla of singlesubs with which to hit the Durgeon craft from both above and below. It was all a matter of strategically repositioning …

A pop-up appeared. With relief Devin saw that it was not the dread safety upgrade. He made a face. He hadn't called for a new character. Nor did he recognize this one. He read the sidebar with interest. A senior officer, no less. The accompanying graphic was impressive, featuring a powerfully-built older man clad in advanced underwater gear. It was unusual, Devin knew, to see a senior officer character dressed for on-field battle. Usually they were only accessible when boardroom strategy was being discussed. He was intrigued.

Even more so when the character removed its rebreather mask and spoke.

It seemed to be looking directly at him.

"Greetings, soldier. I am General Valentin Sharffen and I'm taking command here."

"Whoa!" Devin grinned at the monitor, whose metal frame featured Pollockian stains rendered in tomato sauce and smeared chocolate. "Where'd you come from?"

"Origins are unimportant. The state of battle is. There is more at stake here than you can imagine."

"I know, I know." This bit of character-gamer interface was brilliant, Devin thought. Damn brilliant. "The fate of the Earth, etc., etc."

On-screen, the character nodded approvingly. "You are straight-forward, soldier, and absolutely correct. What is your name?"

"Devin Butler." He was grinning from ear to ear now. "Sir!"

The character smiled. *This is great,* Devin thought. *Was this part of what Gcube wanted to delete from the game?* He couldn't imagine why.

"Are you prepared to receive orders, soldier?"

Devin found himself sitting up straighter in his chair. "Yes, *sir!*" He flinched as there came a crash from the kitchen that reached him even through the game's music, sound effects, and his headset.

An expression of concern crossed the face of General Valentin Sharffen. "Is there a problem, soldier?"

Without hesitation or considering to what he was replying, Devin mumbled softly. "It's Crapon. My stepfather. He's beating on my mom. When he's not beating on her, he beats on me. Blames her for stuff, just beats on me 'cause he can, I think."

Sharffen's expression tightened, his gaze narrowed. "Plainly a coward. I hate cowards. They put their fellow soldiers in peril. They risk success on the battlefield. They are an embarrassment to the species."

"You can say that again." Screaming from the kitchen. His mother. There were knives in the kitchen. Sometimes Devin thought of—but Crapon was a grown adult, and a pretty big man. The probable outcome of Devin's fantasizing, if ever translated into action, was all too predictable. One didn't have to be a gamer to see that. "I wish—I wish I could ..." His voice, pitiable, trailed away.

"I think I perceive your problem, soldier. Perhaps I can help."

Devin's gaze rose to meet the black CG eyes that were peering unblinkingly back at him. He wasn't at all sure what was going on here, but ...

Another player? Another something—else?

"How could you help?"

"Will you trust me, soldier?"

Trust. A word, a condition, that Devin had long ago abrogated to ensure his very survival. He didn't trust anyone, not really. But this— character—wasn't real. It was part of a gaming program. Nothing more. And yet. And yet.

If he was going to trust something, since real people had always let him down, why not trust something that was not real?

He felt funny. Like when his mother had had too much to drink, when she tried to blot out the interminable gloom that had descended over her life like an impenetrable blanket.

"Sure. Why not? Why shouldn't I trust 'you'?"

The character on screen grew ramrod straight. "I'm promoting you to Lieutenant, Devin Butler."

Oh, well, that was kind of neat, Devin mused. A game character was promoting him instead of him promoting a game character. Interesting twist. He saluted.

The image on screen saluted back. "Now," it said as it lowered its right arm. "Go and fetch your miserable excuse of a stepfather."

Devin swallowed. "Here? You want me to bring him in here?" He gestured at his surroundings. "But this is my room. This is all I got."

"Go get him." The character shape was unyielding. "You told me that you would trust me. Tell him there's a problem with your computer. Tell him you need him to help fix it."

Devin laughed in spite of himself. "Fix it? Man, Crapon can't fix a goddamn leaky toilet! He doesn't know anything about computers."

"Tell him." The character image was insistent. "Tell him that your joystick controller is stuck. Tell him you need his strength. To break it loose."

"He'll probably just break it," Devin muttered.

"This is an order—Lieutenant. Instruct him as I have told you."

Shaking his head, wondering what he was doing, Devin pushed back his chair and rose, still gazing at the monitor. "What if he breaks my controller? I won't be able to play Durgeon Invasion anymore. I won't be able to play *any* games."

"Trust me," General Valentin Sharffen said again. "Something will break, but it will not be your controller."

So Devin, dubious and dazed, went hesitantly into the kitchen, and interposed himself between his blubbering mom and raging step-dad, and made the request. It was met with besotted amusement by his stepfather, who raised a big, heavy hand, but did not strike.

"So *you* need *my* help with your damn *computer*?" Carpon chuckled. "That's a goddamn first!"

"The controller arm is stuck," Devin repeated deferentially, still waiting for the first blow to fall. "I need you to try and fix it."

"Oh, I'll fix it! I'll fix it just right!" Smiling crookedly, Carpon shoved the boy aside and lurched toward his room.

Later, after the police and the ambulance had left and while the coroner was still dictating his report, and unbeknownst to all but a handful of teenagers, the war for the future of Earth began in earnest.

About the Author

Alan Dean Foster is the author of 125 books, hundreds of pieces of short fiction, essays, columns reviews, the occasional op-ed for the *NY Times*, and the story for the first Star Trek movie. Having visited more than 100 countries, he is still bemused by the human condition. He lives with his wife JoAnn and numerous dogs, cats, coyotes, hawks, and a resident family of bobcats in Prescott, Arizona.

If You Liked ...
IF YOU LIKED THE FLAVORS OF OTHER WORLDS, YOU MIGHT ALSO ENJOY:

Oshenerth
by Alan Dean Foster

The Taste of Other Dimensions
by Alan Dean Foster

The Gamearth Trilogy
by Kevin J. Anderson

Other WordFire Press Titles by
Alan Dean Foster

Mad Amos Malone

Oshenerth

The Taste of Other Dimensions

Our list of other WordFire Press authors and titles is always growing.
To find out more and to see our selection of titles, visit us at:
wordfirepress.com